LAST SUPPER

LOCUST POINT MYSTERY, BOOK 8

LIBBY HOWARD

CHAPTER 1

"*B*ingo!"

There was a chorus of groans at the cheerful word—groans from everyone except the blonde woman across the aisle from me. She'd won nearly a dozen baskets tonight as well as the first fifty-fifty, which had ended up being almost seventy dollars. Although, in all fairness, the woman had probably spent three hundred dollars on the many bingo cards she had strategically placed around her. Her strategy was clearly paying off—if her goal was to go home with a truckload of basket winnings, that is.

"That woman is a piece of work," Daisy hissed, glaring over at the blonde.

"Who is she?" I asked, following her gaze and wondering what beyond the woman's bingo luck had annoyed my friend.

"Stacy Mellomaker." Daisy rolled her eyes. "Self-absorbed, shallow, entitled, trophy wife."

I blinked in surprise. Admittedly, Stacy Mellomaker appeared to be a walking stereotype of what Daisy had said with her designer leggings, cleavage-enhancing top, glossy blonde locks, and eyelash extensions, but my friend wasn't normally the sort of person to judge someone by their appearance.

I wasn't, either, until this Stacy woman started winning all the baskets at bingo. The thought made me feel immediately guilty. Luck and an annoying smug smile didn't make someone a horrible person.

"I'm sure she's not that bad," I protested.

"Heck, she's not," Olive chimed in. "She nearly got Chip's Cupcakery shut down over that gluten thing a couple months ago."

"She has Celiac disease?" I grimaced, thinking how difficult that must be and what the heck the woman planned to do with the giant basket of cookies she'd just won.

"No, she's on some diet and claimed the gluten-free muffins weren't really gluten free and caused her to bloat. Chip swore up and down there wasn't even a hint of cross contamination, but the damage was done. He almost went under because of that."

"Then there was that screaming fit last week," Kat added.

"The one at Lester's Auto Repair? Or the one at the library? Or the one at the coffee shop?" Daisy asked.

"The one at Sephora over the lipsticks," Kat replied. They all nodded, making me feel like I'd been completely out of the loop gossip-wise.

"Who was she arguing with at the library?" I asked, sneaking a glance at the woman.

"Last week? The new assistant, Molly," Kat replied. "The week before she was yelling at Mrs. Greenway over the selection of children's book at reading time."

"That poor daughter of hers." Olive shook her head.

"Sheyanne," Daisy commented. "With an 'S' instead of a 'C' and an 'a' instead of an 'e', because naming your daughter after a city in Wyoming isn't weird enough unless you switch up the letters a bit."

I blinked in astonishment. This, coming from a woman whose mother had named her after a flower?

"People wonder if she's even Gus Mellomaker's daughter," Kat snipped with unusual cattiness. "Rumor says Stacy's been sleeping with one of the trainers at the gym, and that he's not the first she's screwed around with. Plus, her husband is ancient. The guy's got to be ninety if he's a day. I can't imagine how he could possibly have fathered a child at his age."

Suzette shuddered. "Ugh, I don't want to imagine that."

As horrible as Stacy Mellomaker sounded, I really didn't want to speculate about the nature of her relationship with her husband. I preferred to think that people truly loved one another, fifty or sixty-odd years of age difference aside. Either way, the matter of how their daughter had been conceived was none of my business.

Was the guy really ninety, though? Maybe Kat was exaggerating by thirty years or so.

We settled in for another round of bingo, me taking quick surreptitious looks at Stacy from the corner of my eyes. She really was a beautiful woman with an amazing figure and meticulous grooming. Far more meticulous than I'd ever want to spend my time on. Seemed like a lot of work, all that makeup, hair, eyelash extensions, perfectly flat stomach, and firm thighs.

I'll admit there was a tinge of envy in my thoughts and probably the same envy in my friends' cattiness. But I was close to twice this woman's age and had no desire to put that much effort into my appearance each and every day. Did she look that good while sweating at the gym? Did she even sweat at the gym? Was she doing all that for her husband? In my experience, women that generally put that much effort into their appearance were doing it for everyone but their husbands. Perhaps those rumors of a lover were well founded.

Or maybe she just liked makeup. Sheesh, who was feeling catty now? I watched the woman carefully place her bingo dots then reach into a designer bag with elegant hands, looking around before she pulled out a flask and took a quick, stealthy swig.

The VFW sometimes sold beer and wine, but the bingo fundraisers were strictly iced tea and lemonade. Bringing in booze in a flask with sparkly bling and engraving on the side? It seemed the sort of classless arrogant action that confirmed my friends' opinions. And it also made me wonder who Stacy Mellomaker really was behind the perfect makeup and firm thighs. Alcoholic? Although those I knew in the past who'd had a drinking problem tried very hard to hide their addiction. I couldn't imagine one of them swigging from a flask in a bingo game—at least not without hiding in a bathroom stall or out in their car to do it.

"Bingo!" Stacy raised her hand again, and everyone glared at her.

"Food's ready," Olive announced as one of the assistants began calling out Stacy Mellomaker's winning numbers to verify them. It was pretty much a formality at this point. The woman hadn't gotten an erroneous bingo all night. "Shall we eat, ladies?"

"Let's mug her in the parking lot," Daisy suggested, eyeing the baskets that were filling up Stacy's table. "Or just snatch one as she is loading them in her car. There's no way she'll miss one basket among the three hundred she's won tonight."

"A dozen, not three hundred," I corrected. "Go eat. You're getting grumpy. Or hangry as Henry calls it."

"I missed out on that Cookie Delight basket. Might as

well give bingo a rest and drown my sorrows in pot pie," Daisy grumbled, getting to her feet.

We'd made bingo night at the VFW a monthly event, a sort-of girls' night out. Suzette, Kat, Olive, Daisy, and I would shell out for the raffle tickets and the bingo cards, sometimes heading out afterward for a quick beer. Tonight was a bit different from the typical bingo night. The money was to benefit the volunteer fire department, and in addition to bingo and raffles, the VFW was serving dinner. It was the usual fare—turkey salad sandwiches, sliced ham, baked macaroni and cheese, and chicken pot pie.

The first time I'd ordered pot pie, I'd imagined it would be an actual pie with a top and bottom crust, filled with chicken, gravy, potatoes, and vegetables, but here in Locust Point, pot pie meant something different. I'd been told it was from the German immigrants who'd originally settled in this area. The dish was pretty much chicken and dumplings without the biscuit dumplings on top. Basically, it was chicken broth, tons of shredded chicken, potatoes, and thick dough squares boiled in the broth like chewy noodles. The potato starch thickened the dish up. It was good—hearty and filling, and perfect for a brisk November evening when none of us seemed to be winning at bingo.

Daisy, Kat, and I took a break from the game and went to get food, vowing to bring back bowls for Olive and Suzette who were determined to play on.

"Maybe I'll bring Stacy a bowl of pot pie and accidently dump it across half her bingo cards," Daisy groused.

I looked over at the woman and saw her take a surreptitious drink from the flask before dropping it into her bag and heading on an intercept with us to the food line.

"Crap. Here she comes," Kat hissed. "Hold back. I don't want to have to wait in line standing next to her."

I had no such reservations and was hungry, so I waved

my friends off and continued on, reaching the line just before Stacy Mellomaker.

"Hi," I greeted her. "You're having amazing luck tonight."

She pivoted, her gaze roaming over me before she turned back around. It was as if she'd made an evaluation of my worth and found me lacking.

"That cookie basket is amazing. I think I gained ten pounds just looking at it. Yum," I continued. I'd been a journalist and was now working for an investigation and bail bonds firm. I was nothing if not persistent in the face of rejection.

"I'm keto," she informed me.

I had no idea what being keto meant, but I remembered what Olive had said about Chip's Cupcakery and figured it must have something to do with not consuming gluten. "Well, your daughter will love those cookies, then."

"Baked goods aren't good for children."

I nearly gasped in horror at her comment. True, nobody should consume excessive amounts of sugary baked goods, but the occasional cookie or muffin was part of what made life wonderful.

"I'll probably just throw it away," she added.

"Well, make sure you throw it away into the back seat of the silver sedan in the parking lot," I joked. "I'll properly dispose of the contents in a safe and effective manner."

We fell into an awkward silence as we edged forward a bit at a time. Well, I felt it was awkward. Stacy probably didn't care.

"Do you play bingo often?" I asked, choosing this line of small talk over the other options of weather and plans for next week's Thanksgiving holiday.

"No."

I persisted despite the frosty tone of the word. "So, you're just here for the pot pie? Or to support the volunteer fire department fundraiser?"

She smirked. "Oh, I love the firemen. I'm here for something else though, tying up some loose ends on something. Winning all these baskets from a bunch of toothless trailer trash is just a bonus."

I winced. Most of the women in the room were either professionals with white-collar careers or homemakers, and as far as I could tell we all had more than adequate dental care. My friends were right—this woman truly was horrible.

Which was why I didn't mention that the dough squares in the pot pie were full of gluten as she took a big bowl. Serves her right if she bloated up like a Macy's Thanksgiving Day Parade balloon tonight.

I made my way back to the table, carrying both a bowl of pot pie for myself and another one for Olive. Looking back, I saw that Kat and Daisy were finally getting their own, and that Daisy had picked up an extra bowl for Suzette.

"You're right," I told Olive as I handed her the food. "Stacy Mellomaker is not a very nice person."

Olive took the bowl and nodded. "She call us all hillbillies or something? Snob."

"Close enough. She was critical of our oral hygiene." I sat down and glanced over to see the other woman digging into her pot pie. How she managed to eat and keep track of her slew of bingo cards was beyond me.

"I've got no idea why she's even here," Olive complained. "Bingo doesn't seem highfalutin enough for someone like her."

Why *was* she here? She'd said it wasn't for the bingo or the baskets, and it wasn't over any incredible desire to support fundraising for the volunteer fire department. She was sitting alone, so it's not as if a friend had pressured her into coming. Why was she here?

Kat and Daisy sat down, arranging their space just as a new bingo game began. I lost myself in the joy of warm, filling pot pie, and the excitement of the dots filling up my bingo cards. I was so close to winning this time. "Come on, B8," I muttered to myself.

"Bingo!"

I cringed and turned to see Stacy waving her hand in the air once more.

"Seriously?" Daisy snapped. "I wanted that Terrific Teas basket. Darn it all."

"Eat your dinner," Kat told Daisy. "Try to ignore her and just have fun."

"I've never seen you so upset over losing at bingo," I commented. "Yes, it's annoying that she had something like thirty cards over there and is cleaning up, and she's clearly a jerk, but is there a more personal reason you're giving Stacy Mellomaker the stink eye?"

"I just don't like her. I've never liked her." Daisy scooted her chair so her back was to the other woman. "She's shallow, spiteful, and a cheat."

"How do you cheat at bingo?" I wondered. The machine that selected the numbers seemed pretty tamper-proof. All the cards had equal odds of having a winning combination, although I was pretty sure some of the diehard bingo fans would argue with me on that point. The assistant was reading off the winning combination and verifying them with the woman calling them out. I couldn't imagine how Stacy could possibly be cheating at this game.

"She cheats at other stuff," Daisy grudgingly admitted. "But if she *could* cheat at bingo, I'm pretty sure she would."

"I'll share the Shower Power basket I won," Suzette told Daisy. "There's some nice soaps in there. I know it's not cookies, but you could have the loofa."

"Thanks." Daisy let out a big sigh and stirred her pot pie. "It's not really the bingo game. I just can't stand that woman."

"Well, you're not the only one," Olive told her. "It's not like Matt can ban her from the event though. It's a fundraiser, and she has spent a lot of money on all those cards—far more than she's won tonight. Hopefully she won't make a habit of this and will go back to doing whatever it is she normally does on Tuesday nights."

I decided to ignore the woman, focusing instead on my food. Thankfully the next four baskets did *not* go to Stacy Mellomaker. Daisy finally won a gardening basket and passed it over to me.

"Here. I know you've been coveting this all night. All I ask is that you let me have some basil this summer."

I snatched it up, thrilled with the contents—an assortment of heirloom seeds, a nice spade and three sets of gloves, some bulbs. It was too late to put those bulbs in. I'd need to plant them in the spring and hope for a few late flowers.

"Oh, you're absolutely getting basil and some of these yellow tomatoes if I can get them to grow," I told her. I'd never been all that good at growing tomatoes from seed, but I was willing to give these a try. Maybe I could find it in the budget this year to get myself a little cold frame to acclimate my seedlings this spring. I wish I could put a little greenhouse out back, but that was way out of my budget.

Hmm. How much would a cold frame cost? Perhaps it could be a Christmas present to myself. It would be the first time I'd gotten a Christmas present in ten years.

Eli had been incredible about gifts. He'd put so much thought into picking out the perfect item. Sometimes it was a kitchen gadget that was exactly what I'd been wanting, or a dress I'd been eyeing, but more often than not it was tickets to a show or a weekend skiing upstate, or a cabin getaway in the woods. Eli liked gifting experiences, but after his accident, those experiences had changed to things like a thousand-piece puzzle worked together, or an audio books series that we could listen to each night.

I missed all that. Puzzles and audio books, too.

Out of the corner of my eye I saw Stacy Mellomaker get to her feet. At first, I thought she was returning her dishes to the kitchen, then I realized how absurd that thought was. She was probably headed to the bathroom, although I'd expected she'd try to hold it until the end of this round, especially with a much-coveted Bath Bomb basket up for grabs. She'd already won the Teddy Bear Basket the previous round. I was sure her daughter would like that, although a woman who didn't allow her child to eat cookies probably didn't let her have stuffed animals, either.

A young woman in the back of the hall won the bath-supply basket. I concentrated on the next game, cheering when Suzette won the second fifty-fifty prize and happily pocketed her seventy dollars.

"I'll take your bowl up," Daisy told me as she stood. "Here, play my cards. I'm going to run to the bathroom."

"Hurry back," I replied, pulling Daisy's cards over near me. I wasn't sure how I was going to manage six cards in total. Hopefully she'd pee fast.

I was busy trying to scan for G58 when I heard a shout and the slam of the bathroom door bouncing against the wall.

"Call an ambulance!" Daisy shouted, poking her head out of the restroom.

The room erupted into chaos with several people presumably dialing nine-one-one on their phones, while the rest—me included— ran for the restroom to see what the problem was. As I pushed my way through the crowd, I saw Stacy Mellomaker sprawled across the bathroom floor and Daisy on her knees next to the woman performing CPR.

I wasn't a doctor, but I was scared for the woman. She'd seemed fine earlier, and I hadn't seen her drinking enough to be passed out on the bathroom floor. Besides, Stacy Mellomaker didn't seem like the sort of person who would allow herself to be in a situation where she'd be drunk or high or sick in front of others. No, something catastrophic had happened. A burst appendix. A heart attack. She'd choked on a mint.

Oh, no. The pot pie. What if the gluten thing hadn't been some diet she'd been on but a legitimate health concern? And I hadn't warned her about the dough squares.

Matt appeared, moving people out of the way and motioning everyone back to their chairs and clearing a path for the ambulance people when they arrived. I stood aside but remained, unable to keep from watching as Daisy counted chest compressions and the first responders swarmed the tiny bathroom.

The room was alarmingly silent as the EMTs took over for Daisy. I watched as they shoved needles into the unconscious woman, slapped a mask on her face, and pulled out the defibrillator. One of the EMTs walked up to Daisy and me, asking questions about Stacy's medical history, any medications she might be on, and what she'd eaten.

Daisy ran a shaking hand through her hair. "Pot pie, coffee." She motioned to the tables behind us in the hall. "I think she had iced tea with dinner, but I'm not sure. I don't think she had any food allergies."

"We don't know her well enough to say if she was on any medication or not. Actually, I don't know her at all," I said.

"Can one of you get her purse?" the guy asked. "We'll track down her doctor and medical records, but there might be something in her purse. We need to know right now if she's on anything that might interact with what we're giving her, or that might have caused her medical emergency."

I nodded and took off, snatching Stacy's purse from amid the dozen cellophane-wrapped baskets and taking it back. The man questioning Daisy dug through Stacy's purse, pulling out whole lot of prescription bottles and a little pill case.

Wow. How did a thirty-some-year-old woman need that many pills?

"Nexium, Xanax, Oxycontin, Haloperidol, Depakote," he called out as he took notes. Then the man opened the little pill case and shook his head. "Vitamins. Some herbals." Shoving it all back in the bag, he scooped it up. "Did she have anything else?"

I frowned for a second, feeling like there was something I was forgetting in the shock of all this. "Not that I remember."

"We've got a heartbeat," one of the EMTs announced. A few of the people out in the hall cheered at the words, then we all stood back as the paramedics put Stacy on the stretcher and rushed her out into the waiting ambulance.

The bingo participants and volunteer staff remained in the oddly silent bingo hall and stared at each other in shock. None of us knew what we should do now. Should someone try to reach Stacy's husband? Did anyone know his number? Should we continue playing bingo? Who was going to get Stacy's baskets and take them to her home? These were all the weird, inane questions that went through my brain in the face of such an unexpected emergency.

It reminded me of when I'd gotten the call about Eli's accident, and the one thing I couldn't get out of my mind was the thought that someone needed to cancel his surgical patient for the morning. It's as if while in shock, the human mind tries to anchor itself with mundane logistical concerns.

"Should we continue?" Matt walked up to ask me. "I mean, I hate to be disrespectful when someone just had a medical emergency."

"It's a fundraiser," I told him. "I think you should continue. Maybe ask if someone can take Stacy's winnings home for her?"

"I'll take them," Kat said. "We're not friends or anything, but I know her pretty well, and I know her sister. I know where Stacy lives. We're both on the library fund committee and the church building funds committee together."

I glanced over at Daisy. "You doing okay?"

She shook her head. "Stacy's not… she's not good, Kay. I think she was on the bathroom floor for a while, that she wasn't breathing for at least five minutes. She wasn't responding to CPR, and I know what those paramedics were thinking. Heck, I was thinking the same thing. I tried. I really tried. The woman's thirty-five years old. She's too young to be dead, to have a massive heart attack or a fatal medical emergency like this. It's just…it's just wrong, and terrifying, and I keep thinking about her little girl and her husband, and all the horrible things I was saying about her. And all those medicines…. Goodness, I feel so ashamed."

I reached out and rubbed Daisy's arm, never having seen my friend so distraught. "Let's go. I'll drive and you can stay at my house tonight. I'll drop you back off to get your car in the morning after yoga."

She took a deep breath and let it out. "I'll be okay."

"No, you will not be okay. You're staying at my house tonight. No arguing," I insisted.

"Oh, I know better than to argue with you." She gave me a weak smile. "You'll need to loan me some pajamas, though."

"And a toothbrush. I'm always prepared for a friend sleepover. Now get your purse and let's go."

We said our goodbyes and headed to my car. Daisy was unusually silent as I drove, staring out the window at the dark landscape before us, only lit in the narrow beam of my headlights.

"She's got a four-year-old daughter." Daisy's voice was soft, the words broken with emotion.

I wasn't sure whether to tell Daisy that we should be optimistic, that Stacy might pull out of this and recover or not, so I just made a sympathetic noise and remained quiet.

"Four years old. Her husband is in his eighties. That little girl is going to face losing both her parents before she's in first grade."

"Isn't there a sister? Are they close?" I asked.

Daisy nodded. "Brenda. She and Stacy fight like cats and dogs, but then Stacy fights with everyone. I think the only reason Brenda keeps in regular contact with her sister is because of Sheyanne."

"If the worst happens, she'll at least have her aunt." It wouldn't help with the grief, the fear a young child would feel at losing her mother so young, but at least there would be loving family to take her in and raise her if she ended up an orphan at a young age.

"Thirty-five is too young." Daisy shook her head. "She's too young for this."

I peered over at my friend. "Did you recognize those medicines she was on? Was she terminally ill? Did she have a serious health condition she hid from everyone that might have caused her heart attack?"

At least I assumed it was a heart attack. The woman's heart had definitely stopped, or Daisy wouldn't have been doing CPR, but I knew next to nothing about medical issues beyond the challenges Eli had suffered after his accident and the things that had come up in dinnertime conversation when he'd been a practicing surgeon.

"Nexium is for acid reflux. Heck, I've got a prescription for that."

"You have acid reflux?" I glanced at Daisy in surprise.

She nodded. "Normally it's tied to obesity, eating large

meals and lying down right afterward, stuff like that. I've got a hiatal hernia that causes mine."

My best friend, and I had no idea she had a hiatal hernia. Or what a hiatal hernia was.

"It's not serious." She reassured me with a smile. "I just have to watch my stress levels. Oh, and not drink red wine or coffee, or eat tomatoes, or lemons, or spicy food, or chocolate—"

"You can't have chocolate?" I gasped. "Daisy, why didn't you tell me?"

"Because then you wouldn't make those amazing double chocolate muffins. And I'm not about to stop drinking my morning coffee. They'll need to pry that out of my cold dead hands before I give that one up. As for wine, I try to stick with white. The pills help with the heartburn if I stray too far into the forbidden territory."

I sat silent, thinking I should pick up some decaf and maybe make lemon muffins instead of the double chocolate. No wait, she couldn't have lemon, either.

Daisy put her hand on my shoulder. "I swear, Kay, if you try to serve me decaf or refuse to make those double chocolate muffins, our friendship is over," she teased.

"Okay, okay. Double chocolate muffins it is. I won't hide them and give you oat bran for breakfast tomorrow."

"You better not!" She laughed, then her smile fell. "The other pills…. Anxiety. Painkillers. Depakote is for seizures."

"Oh, God. She was epileptic? Is that what happened? A seizure? But you were doing CPR on her."

Daisy shook her head. "It's also prescribed for the treatment of bipolar disorder. So is Haloperidol. That's the drug that makes me think the Depakote isn't for seizures, but for bipolar. And Xanax is prescribed for anxiety."

I sighed, thinking of all the challenges people faced every day—challenges they kept private and away from the public eye. Daisy not telling me about her acid reflux was one thing, but psychiatric issues had such a stigma. I completely understood why Stacy might not have wanted anyone to know about her illness and treatment.

"I said all those mean things about her," Daisy went on. "I gossiped about her, and all the while she was struggling with mental health issues."

I thought about our conversation over bingo, about Chip's Cupcakery, the library, the gym, about Stacy's comments as we'd stood in line for the pot pie.

"Daisy, mental illness doesn't excuse someone from being a mean jerk," I told her. "Stacy was a horrible person. I'm sorry she had a mental illness. I'm sorry she might not make it through this heart attack. I'm very sorry for her daughter, and her husband, and her sister. But mean is mean. We don't have to tolerate someone who hurts us and others just because they have a mental illness."

"I know. You're right. It just makes me see her in a new light, you know? Everything had to be just so with Stacy. Exact. Perfect. She'd work two days straight on a project and never could accept that others might not be able to put in that level of time or effort. Her short temper. Her irritability."

"It may explain her behavior, but it doesn't excuse it," I said. "If she was on those medicines, then she had regular doctor's appointments and most likely therapy. But even if she was working to control her mental health issue, it doesn't mean the people around her have to stand there and tolerate her abuse."

"You're right." Daisy took a deep breath and stared out the window again.

After a few moments, I broke the silence. "What exactly happened between you and Stacy?" I asked softly. "It's not like you to take such a strong dislike to someone. What happened?"

Daisy gossiped. She was my go-to whenever I wanted the lowdown on anybody in Locust Point, as well as half the people in Milford and the outlying towns in the county. She'd grown up here. She knew everyone. And even if she didn't like someone, she generally got along with them just fine. Daisy was as sunny as her name, and although she was honest in her assessment of people, she tended to see the world through an optimistic lens. This was…this was odd and so unlike her.

She hesitated a moment, then turned to me. "I just started taking over the evening yoga classes at Fitness Forever for Francine while she's on maternity leave. It's just for the last month of her pregnancy and a couple months after she has the baby."

"Wow. Do you get access to the gym when you're an instructor?" I didn't know Francine, but I had heard of Fitness Forever. It was a pricey women's only health club with a pool, personal trainers, and many exercise classes. I'd looked up their website a few years ago, only to realize I couldn't even afford the organic juices they sold, let alone a membership.

"Yes, and let me tell you, that place is incredible. I do laps in the pool after I teach the last yoga class. It's heaven to have access to an Olympic-sized indoor pool. Heaven."

I could only imagine. I shot my friend an envious look, then motioned for her to go on.

"Stacy is a member and practically lives there when she's not off doing some committee work or taking Sheyanne to story time at the library. She's usually there in the afternoons when I'm at work, but occasionally she comes to take an evening class or meet her personal trainer."

I nodded, imagining what it would be like to have a life of

leisure where money wasn't an issue, and work consisted of high-profile volunteer opportunities, social networking, and keeping fit at the gym. It sounded ideal, but I loved my job and was happy that morning yoga with Daisy was my only fitness routine. The grass was definitely not greener. Although I wouldn't refuse if someone offered me a membership to Fitness Forever.

"I came around the corner one night after swimming and saw Stacy bullying Molly. She had the girl trapped against the wall and was inches from her, jabbing her with a finger and obviously furious about something. The poor girl looked terrified, as if she was on the edge of crying."

"Wait." I frowned. "Isn't Molly the girl from the library? Or are there two Mollys?"

"The same Molly," Daisy told me. "She works at the library part time during the weekends and during the week at Fitness Forever picking up towels, cleaning off equipment, and fetching members juices and waters. That sort of thing. She's a good kid. She and her brother were in my youth fitness group when they were in grade school, and she took a Self-defense for Women course I helped put together this past month. I've known her for years."

"Did she go to Locust Point High School?" I asked, wondering if Madison knew her.

"She and her brother graduated from Milford this past spring. Her parents used to live in Washdale, but they moved into Milford when they were teens."

"What in the world would cause Stacy to go off like that on an eighteen-year-old girl?" I asked, outraged and imagining what Daisy's reaction had been.

"I didn't wait to find out. I pushed my way between them and let Stacy have it. Told her she should be ashamed of herself, and that if she had an issue with Molly, she should take it up with management and not harass the poor girl. She started screaming at me to mind my own business, then called me some not-very-nice names. Molly took off, and Stacy and I ended up drawing a crowd, shouting at each other."

"Good for you!" I was always proud at how Daisy stuck up for kids or those who were being taken advantage of. She was always so strong, confident, outspoken. I was too, but in a more subdued way. I would have intervened, but I wouldn't have gotten into a shouting match. Or maybe I would have. The thought of Stacy bullying an eighteen-year-old employee made my blood boil. No wonder Daisy disliked the woman so.

"Well, I nearly got sacked because of it." Daisy chuckled. "Stacy complained to management. The onlookers were shocked, although I think they were more shocked about Stacy's language than my yelling back at her. In the end, the club needs me. I'm the only qualified yoga instructor that's available to fill in for Francine. The members love my classes. And Stacy is generally disliked, to put it mildly. I got a slap on the wrist."

"Stacy should have been thrown out of the club," I protested.

Daisy shrugged. "Money talks. What can you do?"

So true. As I pulled into my driveway, I couldn't help but wonder if Stacy Mellomaker's heart attack was a bit of karma for all the nasty stuff she'd done in life.

CHAPTER 2

We did yoga in the basement the next morning, partially because it was darned cold with frost on the grass, and partly because Daisy didn't have her yoga clothes and had to do her Vinyasas in borrowed pajamas. I could tell she was feeling better, that the night's sleep had softened the edges of her guilt and distress. Still, I remained silent on the topic of what happened at bingo, instead talking about the upcoming holidays and quizzing her on her excruciatingly slow-moving relationship with my boss, J.T. Pierson.

"The pair of you should come over for Thanksgiving," I told her. "The kids will be here. We're planning a big spread. Madison is making sausage chestnut stuffing, and the judge is picking up some oysters."

"That's all I need. Oysters." She laughed. "Count me in. I don't know about J.T., though."

Uh oh. "I thought everything was full steam ahead after your Florida fishing trip."

I'd wondered if something was wrong when Daisy's enthusiastic plans for a romantic evening culminating in the pair of them finally getting physical had never seemed to come to fruition. If they had, I knew she would have told me. But she hadn't. J.T. wasn't moping around the office, so I wasn't sure what had happened. Daisy and I might be close, but I didn't know how to address this topic. "Did you and J.T. ever end up doing it?" or "Haven't you gotten laid yet?" wouldn't be all that unusual for me to ask a best friend, but I knew Daisy was approaching this whole relationship with the tentative fear of someone who'd spent a lifetime as a single woman—a single woman who'd had lots of disastrous prior relationships. I didn't want to see her get hurt. And I figured she'd tell me if something had gone wrong…or if something had gone right.

"It *was* full steam ahead. Then he was gone a week at that conference, and when he came back…I don't know. I guess I felt like we were back to square one, like we'd lost momentum or something."

"Are you no longer interested in him romantically?" I was so confused.

"Yes. No. I don't know. Everything was incredible in Florida. Then when he got back from the conference, I just felt awkward and wondered if I'd imagined how I'd felt before. We've been dating, but…"

My muscles protested in the extended downward dog pose and I shifted my weight a bit. "Daisy, you're driving me nuts with this indecision. J.T. is a saint—a very patient saint. Do you still like spending time with him?"

"Yes, but—"

"Are you still attracted to him physically?"

"Yes, but—"

"Then for Pete's sake, take the man to bed and enjoy the heck out of some good sex."

"What if it's bad?" Daisy blurted out. "What if we have sex and it ruins everything?"

"Sometimes the first time with someone *isn't* all that great. You know that. It's awkward, and you're both nervous, and it's hard to relax—especially when you've been building up to this for *months* like you both have. You don't want to break up with him, do you?" Break up with him. It sounded like they were both still in high school.

"No!" Daisy protested. "I lo—I like him. I just don't want to ruin everything."

"Being in limbo forever is going to ruin everything. Relax. Make out a lot and see where it goes. J.T.'s a good guy. And you're both experienced adults. Bad sex is fixable when two people are willing to listen to each other and try different things. And I really doubt it will be bad."

I couldn't believe I was having this discussion with Daisy. Actually, I *could* believe I was having this discussion with Daisy, only the roles seemed like they should have been reversed. My friend should have been the one urging me to take a chance, to go out on a limb and risk everything for love, and I should have been the one angsting over what may or may not happen. This was so weird, this role reversal.

"And one more thing—can we get out of this downward dog before my hamstrings explode? I'm dying, Daisy." I huffed out a pained breath to clearly illustrate my situation.

She laughed and moved into Tadasana. "Okay. I'll invite him to come with me here for Thanksgiving. And I'll start giving him the green light again."

I followed her lead, wincing as I stood. "Good. Drag that man off to bed and rock his world. All night long. Have so much sex that you call me and cancel our yoga the next morning because you can barely walk."

Daisy's gaze drifted over my shoulder and I heard the creak of a stair. Spinning around, I saw Judge Beck standing on the bottom step, his eyebrows raised, a look of unholy mirth on his face.

My face blazed hot.

"I'm just going to go back upstairs and get some coffee and a couple of those muffins, if that's all right." He struggled to keep from grinning and failed. "And Daisy? I concur with what Kay said. You should most definitely 'go for it.'"

With that, he turned around and headed back up to the kitchen.

"I'm absolutely mortified," I whispered to Daisy.

"*You?* I just had a judge tell me to go get laid. I guess that means I have to do it now. It's a legal mandate that I sleep with J.T. I don't want to be in contempt of court or anything."

Call me a complete coward, but I endured an additional thirty minutes of yoga rather than go up and face Judge Beck. I listened carefully for the creaking floor sound of him making his way upstairs, and when I was sure he'd begun his shower, we ended our marathon yoga session and headed up for coffee and muffins. Daisy threw on last night's clothes and ran home to shower and change, and I headed upstairs to do the same, well aware that my avoidance would make me late to work—especially since I needed to drop Daisy off at the VFW to pick up her car.

J.T. was in the office when I arrived, and he greeted me with a smile. I eyed him closely, trying to discern anything I could see that would result from a crack in his and Daisy's relationship, but saw nothing but my usual cheerful boss.

"We've got a full schedule today." He handed me a file. "Lots of skip traces. It's typical this time of year. People always get overextended as the holidays approach and put off some bills. Get ready for January. That's when we'll really get slammed."

I wrinkled my nose. "Anything else? Bail bond applications I need to check? A divorce case I can work on? A murder or two or three?" It's not that I didn't want the work, but day after day of skip traces got boring. I longed for something else. Maybe not murder, but something else.

"Not this week." J.T. grinned. "Unless you'd like to play a part in my next video production."

I wasn't *that* bored. J.T. "Gator" Pierson had his own YouTube channel where he hosted weekly dramatic reenactments of local crimes. He'd quickly run out of interesting cases from his investigative agency and since weekly videos of skip traces weren't all that exciting, he'd taken to highlighting crimes in general. Either way, a starring role in his video usually involved me being a victim, or a drug dealer's mom, or an alarmed witness. I was no actress, and after a few episodes, I had informed J.T. that unless he was paying me overtime, my days as a thespian were over.

"Nope. I'll stick with the files, thank you very much," I told him.

"You sure? It involves a car chase."

I blinked, envisioning my boss flying down the back roads in a Jeep. "How are you managing that one?"

He grinned sheepishly. "Photoshop for some of it. Some shots I'll just speed up in MovieStudio so it looks like we're going super-fast."

J.T.'s productions were low budget—very low budget? They'd exploded in popularity with some of the high-profile cases in Locust Point this year, like Holt Dupree's, although I think that many of the people who subscribed to "Gator's" channel tuned in for the B-movie factor and to see their friends and co-workers in guest starring roles.

"Well, have fun," I told him, turning to my desk. "Oh, and before I forget, you and Daisy are invited to Thanksgiving dinner at my house."

There. Now there was no way Daisy could chicken out of it.

"Thank you. I was just going to do something small at

home but hadn't checked with Daisy yet. I'll call her, then let you know."

Hmm, that didn't sound like a man who thought he was getting dumped or was concerned about the stop-go of the physical part of their relationship. Maybe Daisy was the only one freaking out over this. J.T., as usual, seemed perfectly content to go at any pace Daisy set. But I had no time to concern myself further with my boss and my best friend's relationship this morning. I had work to do.

J.T. headed out to film his video, telling me that he had a client to meet afterward and not to expect him back. I assured him I'd lock up and settled in for a long day at my desk. Lunch came and went. I popped down to the corner deli for take-out, bringing a sandwich and a bag of chips back to eat in front of my computer. When the door chimed, I started in surprise, then looked up, hoping that we had a client, or that Miles had come by to visit. Anything but another hour of these skip traces.

It wasn't Miles or a client at the door. It was Matt.

Matt Poffenberger and I had an easy friendship that had started when I'd bought an antique sideboard from an estate auction at his parent's home and gone on to solve an old family mystery. I helped him with some of his charity endeavors, visited his father with him over at the nursing home once or twice a month, and met him here and there for coffee and lunch. All completely platonic.

"I thought you were a client." I motioned him over to one of the chairs. "I've never been so thrilled to see anyone before in my life. Save me from these skip traces. I'm drowning in internet searches right now."

"Sadly, I might actually be a client. I was hoping to run something by you and see what you thought."

I set the files aside and swiveled my chair around to face him. "What's up?"

He sighed. "This thing with Stacy Mellomaker, that's what's up."

I winced. "Is she trying to sue you or something? I mean, it's horrible that she got carted out in an ambulance before the last round, but I can't see how an exciting run of luck at bingo could lead to a heart attack. And even if it did, you'd hardly be to blame."

"All I know is that I had a police detective visiting me this afternoon asking me all sorts of questions."

Oh, poor Matt! He worked so hard at his various organizations and charities. I made a sympathetic noise and scooted closer. "It was probably just routine."

But why would it be routine? Police detectives didn't investigate heart attacks unless someone was claiming it was a result of...I don't know, drugs in their pot pie or something.

"I'm worried, Kay. The detective wanted a list of all the attendees of the bingo night as well as the VFW volunteers working in the kitchen and the bingo game. There were a lot of questions about what Stacy ate, if she got it herself or if someone brought it to her, who had contact with her last night."

I shook my head in confusion. "The woman is crazy. Kat told me what she did with Chip's Cupcakery. I hope she's not going to start a smear campaign against you or accuse one of the volunteers of something." For a second, I thought back on a case I'd recently investigated. "Did she think she was poisoned? Something in her food that might have caused her cardiac arrest? I'll admit thirty-five does seem young for that sort of thing. Maybe she's just being vindictive. Or paranoid. Although she probably has a good reason to be paranoid from what I've been told."

"I'm worried that's what the detective was thinking. I couldn't answer a lot of their questions, but I did have the list of volunteers and attendees and a rough idea where a few people were sitting, but beyond that, I just didn't know." He grimaced. "They might contact you as well. And I'm sure they'll want to talk to Daisy since she's the one that found Stacy in the bathroom and administered CPR."

I remembered my friend's dislike of the woman. "Surely they can't have thought *Daisy* would have caused her heart attack? Or had anything to do with it?"

He shrugged. "I don't know. That detective was really cagey about giving me any information. He asked questions, and I answered them."

"You said you might end up being a client." I winced. "You don't mean the bail bonds side of the business, do you?"

"I hope not. I was thinking more of the investigative work —*your* investigative work, specifically. I want to know what happened. And I want to know if someone at the VFW was involved in that woman's sudden illness. I'd rather be active about all this than just sit back and wait for the police to arrest someone in the middle of a dinner or a bingo night. I know I'm sounding callous here with a woman in the hospi-tal, but I don't want the VFW to look bad. If a volunteer was involved, I want to find out and be the one who presents that information to the police."

I nodded, understanding that this could potentially be a PR nightmare for a man who did a lot of good in our community.

"I'll check into it. What was the detective's name?"

"I've got his card here somewhere." Matt fumbled though his pockets, finally pulling it out and handing it to me.

I read the card, my heart sinking at the familiar name. "Detective Desmond Keeler, Milford Police Department."

CHAPTER 3

I pressed on later than usual, trying to power my way through all the skip trace work. When I got home, Taco greeted me at the door with a chirping sound, purring as he wound his way around my legs. I scooped him up, giving him a quick cuddle before letting him outside. This was our new routine. Taco got some freedom when I got home from work, always returning in a half hour for his all-important bowl of Happy Cat kibble. After letting him out, I hung my coat in the closet and made my way through the foyer, noticing that Judge Beck was in the kitchen making spaghetti, and the kids were at the dining room table doing their homework.

"What can I do to help?" I asked, coming into the kitchen after waving a greeting to Madison and Henry.

"Nothing. I've got it." The judge pointed a spoon at the noodles boiling in a pot. On the next burner was a sauce pan with what I was pretty sure was premade spaghetti sauce being heated up. I looked over and saw two empty glass jars sitting in the sink to be rinsed out and stuck in the recycling bin.

"Did you add sausage and some spices to that?" I didn't want to complain. It was nice to come home to have dinner nearly ready, but the sauce he was using was bland to say the least.

"Oregano and basil and a little garlic salt. I cut up some hot dogs and stuck them in it as well." He laughed at my expression. "I'm joking. Yes, I browned sweet Italian sausage and sliced it up. I'll add it once this is warm."

Yum. Sounded downright edible.

"Madison wanted to make meatballs," he added, "but she's got a calculus exam tomorrow, so I told her no."

"Calculus. Yikes. What's Henry working on?" I got out the bag of Happy Cat and filled Taco's bowl.

"A report on ancient Egypt. How was your day today?"

I loved this. I loved coming home to a family that brought warmth and joy to my evening, people that actually were interested in how my day went. After Eli had died, I'd thought that was gone forever, that the only thing I'd be coming home to was Taco.

I adored my cat, but it was heavenly to have human companionship, people I cared about to share dinner with and make this house a home.

"Skip traces—mostly for Credicorp, but we've got a new client and there were a dozen for them as well. I worked through lunch." Shoving the bag of cat food back in the cupboard, I then looked in the fridge and took out some ingredients to throw together a quick basic salad.

The judge smiled over at me. "Back to the drudgery while J.T. chases down bail jumpers and repos cars?"

"No bail jumpers or repos so far. We're pretty low on the excitement scale right now. J.T. went out to film his video for the week, then headed over to see a potential client."

Well, there'd been no excitement today, but I'd had plenty last night. As if reading my mind, Judge Beck nodded at the Gardening Goodies basket I'd left on the kitchen island.

"Looks like you had some luck at bingo," he commented.

"Not me. Daisy won that one and was kind enough to let me have it. Suzette won a basket and a fifty-fifty, and Kat texted me to say she won the raffle which was a dinner out at that new steakhouse. Daisy and I had left by then. Did you hear the news? About Stacy Mellomaker? She won most everything last night. We were all thinking of ways to jinx her, but then she had what we think was a heart attack. They took her out in an ambulance."

His eyes widened and he laughed. "Good grief, Kay. What did you all do? Curse the woman? Stick pins in a voodoo doll or something?"

"Daisy was contemplating knocking her down in the parking lot and taking one of the baskets, but that's as far as our plotting went." I shook my head. "Stacy seems to be a horrible person, but I'll admit I did feel bad for her."

"I'm sorry your girls' night out was such a bust," the judge said.

"Me too." I nodded. "Although, aside from Stacy's heart attack and the bad luck as far as bingo winnings went, it was fun. Dinner was really good. They had pot pie."

He grimaced. "I never understood the appeal of that stuff. It's so bland."

"It's hearty and filling, and a bit of a local staple," I countered. "What was your day like?"

"Sentencing and approving plea bargains. There's a case we're getting down to the wire on as far as a plea deal, so I might be overseeing jury selection tomorrow or not. I'm thinking not, but you never know."

I finished cutting the tomatoes then threw them into the bowl of lettuce with some pre-shredded carrots. "Matt stopped by this afternoon. Seems he had a visit from Detective Keeler today about Stacy's episode last night. He wanted a list of attendees and volunteers and a bunch of other information. Matt's worried that Stacy's going to sue or claim the VFW was negligent and caused her heart attack in some way."

"She's accusing them of poor sanitation practices? Sudden onset food poisoning that lead to a cardiac arrest?" The judge shook his head. "That's more an issue for the health department. Or a civil case. Not the sort of thing I'd expect a detective with Milford's Major Crimes Division to be getting involved with."

"I know. I was thinking the same. But she's got money—or rather, her husband's got money. Maybe he and the police chief are buddies. Stacy *does* seem to make enemies everywhere she goes. I guess someone like that would easily take the leap to thinking she was intentionally poisoned. She's only thirty-five, and she looks like a fitness model. I know this sort of thing happens sometimes, but she's not the person I'd expect to have a heart attack at her age and level of physical health."

"You never know about people's family histories or latent issues." Judge Beck poured the spaghetti sauce into a bowl, then turned to me. "Wait…she's Gus Mellomaker's wife? *Gus?* He's got to be pushing ninety. His wife is thirty-five?"

I smirked. "May-December marriages. They've been all the rage for the last two millennia, you know. Yes, she's married to Gus Mellomaker. They have a four-year-old daughter, I'm told."

He shook his head in amazement. "You're joking. I'm surprised *he's* not the one in the hospital with a heart attack. How does he keep up with her?"

I grabbed the bowl of salad in one hand and the noodles in the other. "Probably with lots of Viagra."

Before he could reply, I'd fled the kitchen for the safety of the dining room where the kids were scooting their books aside and moving plates and silverware into position. I didn't know what had gotten into me lately. First my bold conversation with Daisy this morning and now joking around with Judge Beck about Gus and Stacy Mellomaker's sex life.

"I'll go call Taco in for dinner," Madison told me as she headed for the front door.

We all sat down to eat spaghetti and salad with Taco crunching away at his food in the kitchen. The sauce was surprisingly good, and I vowed never to doubt Judge Beck's ability to turn pre-prepared food into a tasty dinner again. When we were done, I volunteered to do the dishes, knowing that the kids needed time for their studies and that the judge had most likely brought work home as well.

Cleanup was a breeze thanks to my newly purchased, refurbished dishwasher that most definitely didn't match anything in my kitchen and stood out like an ugly wart on a beauty queen. But the appliance that I'd purchased used worked reliably, and I was grateful that we were no longer washing everything by hand.

Finally done, I snuck past my roommates hard at work at the dining room table and cuddled up with Taco in the parlor, my knitting on my lap. Eli's ghost materialized in his usual spot—a filmy, shadowy figure visible out of the corner of my eye. He wasn't appearing as often as he had in the past, and I had mixed feelings about that. I wasn't ready to let him go; I wasn't ready to live without the comfort of his spirit. I still craved this gossamer touch of his presence, reminding me of all the years we'd shared together. I was terrified to go on without him.

And I knew how very unfair that was. I didn't want to be the one holding him back from a peaceful afterlife. He'd endured a lot in the last ten years of his life. To cling to him, to deny him his rest, was selfish. I longed for the night when he no longer appeared and I'd know he had journeyed beyond this world, yet I was flooded with relief every time I saw his shadowy form and felt him near.

"Welcome home," I whispered to the ghost. "I'm finishing up a scarf for Olive tonight. The ones for Daisy, Suzette, and Kat are already done. I've got one more for Madison, then if I have time, I thought I'd make one for Violet and one for her to take in to Peony. I'm not sure if she's allowed presents or not. I hope so."

I'd thought about Peony a lot over the last few months. Her plea deal had finally gone through, and thankfully she hadn't ended up being tried as an adult. It seemed the delay allowed the media frenzy over the incident to cool down, and the prosecutor's office had backed off a bit. She'd pled guilty to manslaughter and a possession charge and would be out of the juvenile detention center this coming summer after serving a year. She'd then face two years' probation.

I wasn't sure what the future held for the girl and that worried me. After she'd served her time, would she go back to her family's house where multiple convictions seemed to be the norm? What would school be like for her next year— her senior year? I knew she was taking classes while at the detention center, but would she attend Locust Point High School next year or drop out? I couldn't imagine it would be easy for her to go back to school with everyone knowing what she'd done.

The girl would be facing a fork in the road of her life. Would she take the path her sister Violet had or the path the rest of her family seemed to wander down?

I completed Olive's scarf and started in on Madison's, eventually hearing the kids announce their goodnights and climb the stairs. Taco wandered off to patrol the house, then came back to curl up by my side as I knitted. Keeping track of the pattern, I thought about Peony, about Daisy and J.T., about Matt, and about Stacy Mellomaker. Eventually I realized the swirl of thoughts filling my mind weren't going to resolve themselves this evening, and I might as well go upstairs. Putting the knitting safely away from Taco's paws, I went into the dining room. By now the kids would be fast asleep, but Judge Beck was still up and still sitting at the table, files and folders spread out all around him.

"Are you going to bed soon?" I asked. "I think I'm going to head on up."

"No, I've probably got another hour before I call it a night." He glanced up at me, and something in his expression made me hesitate. "I…I, uh, want to ask you something and I'm not sure how to do it without it sounding odd or putting you in an awkward position."

"Well, that sounds intriguing." I came in and sat down opposite him. "Ask away."

"Remember I told you a few weeks ago that my name was put in for an opening at the state appellate court?"

I nodded.

"Remember when I said a lot of advancement in this job is through rubbing elbows with people, socializing with colleagues and people of influence?"

I eyed him skeptically. "I don't know anybody of influence, so if you're wanting me to put a word in for you, I won't be of much help."

"No, it's not that. I haven't gone to a lot of these events since Heather and I split up. I do the golf outings, and there are meetings and conferences and things like that, but there are a lot of social functions where it would be…awkward for me to attend by myself."

Was he asking me to go to a party with him? No, that was ridiculous. He wouldn't want his landlady, a woman fifteen years his senior, to go to a lawyer-judge-politician party. He probably wanted me to watch the kids or something while he took some twenty-five-year-old supermodel to the important party. Yes, I was sure that was it.

Or maybe he wanted me to set him up with someone to take to the party? I quickly ran through all the young, single women of my acquaintance and realized it was a short list.

"I need someone who can carry on an intelligent conversation with professionals, someone who knows the politics of these things and isn't going to say or do the wrong thing. I need someone who isn't going to spur rumors that I'm running around like a middle-aged playboy. If Madison was five years older, I'd take her, but she's too young to handle this sort of thing, and I'm not about to ask Heather to go with me. We can barely stand to be in the same room long enough to hand off the kids, let alone go to a party together. So, would you?"

I blinked at him. "Would I what? Watch the kids while you go? Sure, I'd love to."

"No. Would you go with me? It's at the capitol, so it's a bit of a drive. It's Sullivan, Morris, Stein, and Callahan's annual Christmas party. Everyone with any influence whatsoever is invited. And with me being up for this position, I feel like I really should attend. But not alone. With you."

"With *me*?" Was I just really tired, or not hearing him right? Because it sounded like Judge Beck had just invited me to go to a swanky Christmas party with him. As his date. Or not-date.

"Kay, you're smart and sophisticated. You'll know what to say and what not to say, and how to deal with snarky backstabbing people or people trying to pry for dirt."

"You make it sound so appealing."

He sighed, running a hand through his hair. "The food is amazing. There's a band and dancing. And booze. Lots of booze."

"If I drink the booze, I won't be able to fend off all the backstabbing gossipy people."

He laughed. "Okay, it does sound horrible."

"I'll go," I told him. "But you owe me one. Quid pro quo here, buddy. You're going to have to accompany me to some horrible event in the future as a payback, you know? I'm warning you that this future event may involve yoga and cats, or a three-hour lecture on marzipan and puff pastry."

He grinned. "Deal. The party isn't until mid-December, so you've got time to get a dress and a hair appointment, or whatever it is you women do to prep for these things."

A dress. I wasn't quite Cinderella, but there was a rather limited amount of formal wear in my closet, most of which was about fifteen years old. Or older.

"Black tie? White tie? Standard evening attire?" I asked, holding my breath that this wouldn't be too formal.

"Black tie."

Ugh. Full length. I could probably get away with an appropriately dressy cocktail length dress, but I didn't want to chance it in a room full of backstabbing, prying people. I'd need to see what I had upstairs in the closet that still fit. And if nothing fit, then I was going to have to go on a borrowing spree among friends and neighbors who might wear the same dress size as me. That or fess up to Judge Beck that I couldn't afford a gown for a one-time event.

No, I was sure I had something. Eli and I had attended plenty of formal events back in the day, and my weight hadn't changed that much over the years. If I needed to, I could do a three-week grapefruit diet or something to fit into what I had.

Darn. Maybe I shouldn't have eaten that pot pie or had that second helping of spaghetti tonight.

$\mathcal{D}$aisy and I cut our yoga short the next morning. I'd made the mistake of telling her right when she'd arrived about Matt's visit, warning her that Detective Keeler may be paying her a visit, and she instantly lost her yoga-inspired calm and centered stance. We headed up to the kitchen before dawn and settled in with coffee and a cinnamon pecan loaf while the rest of the house still slept.

"Why would he want to talk to me?" Daisy fussed, shifting with agitation in her chair. I eyed her coffee, wondering if I should offer to put some brandy in it.

"It might be nothing," I tried to reassure her. "Matt didn't even know why Detective Keeler was questioning him."

"She's probably going to sue." Daisy scowled. "Or go on some horrible social media campaign like she did with Chip's Cupcakery. The VFW raises a lot of money on pancake breakfasts, bingo, and pot pie dinners. They don't need rumors of heart attack-inducing botulism. Matt does a lot of good in this community. It's wrong to blame his volunteers or the VFW for this. Wrong."

"I know, I know." I waved my hand to try to calm her.

"And how in the world could they think *I* could have anything to do with her heart attack?" Daisy glared at her coffee, as if it were Detective Keeler himself. "Yes, Stacy and I had that very vocal argument in the gym. Yes, I made no secret of the fact that I hated Stacy Mellomaker. But I helped her. I was the one who found her, called for help, and administered CPR. What? Do they think I injected her with something in between chest compressions? Slipped a cyanide capsule into her mouth while doing artificial resuscitation?"

"I don't know, Daisy. I don't know what Detective Keeler is thinking, or even why he's handling this and not telling Stacy she needs to go to health and safety inspections or hire an attorney for a civil suit. It's not like it's a homicide or anything."

I got a sick feeling as I said the words. What *was* Detective Keeler doing on this "case"? Stacy was going to be okay, wasn't she? The news hadn't reported otherwise yesterday, but then again, I knew that hospitals and police could hold back on announcements if they had good reason. What if she *had* died, and they hadn't released that information to the public yet? What if she was in a coma and not expected to come out? Brain dead and on life support? From what Daisy had said that night, it wouldn't be too much of a stretch.

But a heart attack? I made a mental note to do some research on what sort of medications, or herbs, or drugs could cause someone to have a massive heart attack. Or what might interact with the medications we knew Stacy was taking and cause cardiac arrest. Whether this was just some cockamamie nonsense Stacy had dreamed up to point the finger at an imaginary enemy, or someone had actually facilitated her illness or possibly even death, I should check it out. I owed it to Matt and to Daisy to find out what was going on.

And I was nosy. That was my primary motive, I'll confess.

And nosiness was closely followed by anything that might alleviate the boredom of that huge stack of skip traces.

Daisy sighed. "I guess you're right. I shouldn't be freaking out over all this. There are a dozen people I can think of off the top of my head who would have motive to put Stacy in the hospital. I might be one of those people, but I'm hardly the only one."

"Besides," I told her, "it's not like disliking someone is a motive for poisoning or whatever, for normal people. If you had a history of road rage or attacking people who cut in front of you in line or sending hate mail and stalking people who took the last of the coffee and didn't make more, then maybe you'd be a suspect."

She laughed. "Well, at least I've got that going for me. I'll admit I get angry when I see someone wronged or hurt, but I don't take it to extreme or fly off the handle for little stuff."

I toasted her with my coffee mug. "Then let's not let this whole thing ruin our morning."

* * *

SADLY, this whole thing *was* about to ruin our morning.

I went to slide into my car and caught sight of a shadow out of the corner of my eye. It was a ghost, firmly ensconced in the passenger seat, and it wasn't Eli.

I ignored her and started my car. Yes, *her*. The ghost was no more than an indistinct form, but I somehow knew this spirit was female. Ghosts tended to visit me when they'd died either at another's hand or with unresolved business. I wasn't ruling out that another woman had died with unfinished business in the county, but I suspected this ghost was Stacy Mellomaker.

Which meant the woman had died. At least, I thought the presence of her spirit meant that. I guess she could have been experiencing some sort of astral projection or perhaps was in a coma, but I was going with death.

"I'm sorry you didn't make it," I told the ghost as I began to back out of the driveway. "I'm sorry for your family, especially your little girl. I'm sorry you died at such a young age. But I'm not going to help you pin your death on some innocent person you had a beef with at the gym, or the library, or at the bakery, or one of Matt's volunteers. So take a hike and head toward the light."

The radio came on, the digital readout of the channel flipping around until it settled on one. "Tragedy" by the Bee Gees filled my car.

"Yes, it's a tragedy. Now go away." I turned out of my street and headed toward downtown.

The station switched and B.J. Thomas crooned "Another Somebody Done Somebody Wrong Song." I loved this song so I head-bopped along for a bit before commenting to the ghost. "Gus was leaving you and wanted a divorce?" I finally asked. "Or the trainer at the gym you were fooling around with told you to shove off?" That's what the song lyrics were, so I was assuming Stacy's unfinished business had to do with her love life.

I felt her irritation and the station changed again. Fleetwood Mac's "Blood on the Floor" came on. I didn't know this one well, so I had to listen to a few bars to get the gist of the song.

"No one shot you, Stacy," I told the ghost. "You can't tell me you were murdered. You had a heart attack."

The volume got louder, and I winced, reaching forward to turn it down. "Okay, so you think you were murdered. Was it your husband because he caught you cheating? A spurned lover? Colonel Mustard in the library with a candlestick?"

The station changed again, and I found myself listening to "Murder by Numbers" by The Police.

"Random unknown killer then," I mused. "Listen, Stacy, from what I've been told, I'm sure a lot of people wanted you to leave town, move to another state, or just stay out of their lives forever. As horrible a person as you were, that doesn't mean someone murdered you. You had a heart attack. I'll admit it's not common to hear that a fit woman died at the age of thirty-five from a heart attack, but things happen. And from the contents of your purse, you certainly weren't free from medical issues. It's time to accept no one was to blame for your death besides cruel fate and move on to your afterlife."

The channel changed again, this time to the news.

"A local woman collapsed Monday while playing bingo at the local VFW, only to die at the hospital. Stacy Mellomaker, wife of real-estate developer Gus Mellomaker, was only thirty-five years old and leaves behind a young daughter in addition to her husband. She was well known for chairing several committees and heading prominent projects in Milford, including the library expansion and beautification plan, the Downtown Historic Preservation Committee, as well as her position on the board of the Rose Allen Memorial Art Museum. She will be sadly missed."

I was sure she would be missed by some people. Her daughter. Her husband. There had to be people who Stacy had worked with that admired her energy and dedication, who hadn't gotten on the wrong side of her temper. I was sure the ghost of the woman sitting next to me had *some* friends who were grieving right now along with her family. And her sister…. I had no siblings of my own, but I could imagine that even the most contentious of sibling relationships still held a core of love underneath it all. Her sister must be grieving as well.

But that didn't mean I was going to go on a crusade trying to find someone to blame for a death that had been by natural causes. I thought back to Monday night, to the image of Stacy sprawled across the bathroom floor, of Daisy with her mouth tightened into a grim line as she did chest compressions.

A fatal heart attack at thirty-five. The woman might have been horrible to that Molly at the gym and intolerable to a ton of others in the community, but no one deserved to have their life cut short so young.

And what if…. I thought about Matt and his visit from Detective Keeler. The family and the police must think there was foul play involved. Had her pot pie been poisoned? I frowned, trying to remember who'd handed her the bowl of food. Had one of Matt's volunteers managed to quickly slip something in the bowl before handing it to her and do it without being seen? Or had the whole batch been tainted and we were all fine because we weren't on a medicine that might have adversely reacted to the poison? How the heck would the murderer have known no one else was taking those specific drugs, though? I couldn't imagine a killer being so careless as to poison one woman and gamble on almost a hundred other lives. If he or she really were that desperate and insensitive, then why poison? Why not just stab her in the parking lot? Or bludgeon her in the bathroom?

What was I thinking? I didn't know this woman. I'd spent five minutes in line talking to her at the bingo game and that hadn't been a pleasant experience. Let the police handle this. If there was foul play involved, they'd figure it out. If not, then the ghost next to me needed to go haunt someone else.

The channel switched again, and I heard Huey Lewis singing "Doing It All for My Baby."

A four-year-old daughter. My heart twisted at the thought, but I still wasn't going to get involved. Let Detective

Keeler handle this one. I had enough to do with all the skip traces I had piled up on my desk.

I parked and headed into the office, leaving the ghost of Stacy Mellomaker behind, still sitting in the passenger seat of my car.

J.T. was inside already working at his desk, and he'd brought a dozen bagels and cream cheese to go with our coffee this morning.

"What's this?" I asked, pulling a pumpernickel bagel from the bag. "Is there a special occasion or something?"

"I know you stayed through lunch yesterday, so I thought I'd at least have something here for you to snack on if you end up doing the same today." He grinned sheepishly. "Those skip trace files…I appreciate you working so hard on them, Kay. I know you'd rather be out investigating something."

"I *am* investigating something. I'm investigating people skipping out on their student loans and credit card debt. Yes, I'd love a bit of variety, but spending my day tracking down people on the internet is more fun than sitting outside a hotel room for hours trying to catch a cheating spouse."

J.T. shook his head. "I miss the good old days sometimes, when a skip trace used to involve questioning neighbors and following people around, when it was like the *Rockford Files* and *Ellery Queen*."

"*Columbo* or *Barnaby Jones*," I added.

"*Kojak*." J.T. arched an eyebrow and shot me a sideways look. "Who loves ya, baby?"

I laughed. "That lollypop he always had in his mouth. Freud would have had a field day with that."

"I had a huge crush on Angie Dickenson. *Police Woman*— now that was a great show."

I rolled my eyes. "She spent most of her days impersonating prostitutes and going undercover in porno flicks. I'll admit I was happy to see a woman in a starring role where she wasn't a homemaker, but I wish they'd focused as much on the detective part of the plot as the sex appeal of their main character."

J.T. shrugged. "Not like *Charlie's Angels* was any better."

"Let's not judge serial crime shows by those yardsticks, shall we? *Baretta* never went undercover as a male prostitute or spent his time ducking bullets while his partner did the heavy lifting."

"Okay." J.T. lifted his hands. "You're right. But in my defense, I was seventeen. And you've got to admit having a woman in that sort of role was rare at the time. Plus, she was forty, wasn't she? How often, even now, do you see a woman that age being portrayed as sexy?"

He was right, although it was more common now than all those years ago. Sheesh, if women over thirty were considered no longer sexy, then what would society think of a woman my age?

I knew exactly what society thought of women my age. Matronly. Grandmother-like. Not sexy. Or if they were sexy, it was as a caricature, someone to make the viewers wince or laugh at. Did anyone think that Blanche Devereaux was sexy beyond the seventy-year-old guys she hit on in the *Golden Girls* show? Were twenty-something men drooling over her?

"So, what was *your* favorite detective show from the seventies?" J.T. asked.

I thought on that one. "Probably *Hart to Hart*. Although if we dip into the 80s, I really liked *Remington Steele* and *Moonlighting*. Early *Moonlighting*, before they actually started sleeping with each other."

He nodded thoughtfully. "Couple detectives. I'm sensing a theme here, Carrera. Is it that your strong female lead actually needs a male sidekick to get the job done? Or the romance subplot?"

I laughed. "With *Hart to Hart*, I liked how their marriage

was portrayed. After all those years, they were still so much in love and so very attracted to each other. In *Remington Steele*, the things women had to do to make themselves seem credible in a man's world resonated with me. As for *Moonlighting*, I loved the witty banter. The romance was fun, but not a key component of my viewing pleasure. Like I said, I would have liked *Moonlighting* a whole lot better if the two main characters had never actually gotten together."

"Well, these days it's less feet-on-the-street and more digging around people's lives via computer." J.T. pushed a stack of folders over to me. "Here's today's work."

My heart sank. "I still have half of yesterday's files to do."

He smirked. "Hence the bagels. I'm off to talk to a few potential corporate clients about picking up their business, so I won't be back until this afternoon."

Great. "Bring back a clone while you're at it. Or a second employee to help with all this. If we pick up any more skip tracing contracts, I'll be working twenty-four seven."

He picked up his coat and grabbed his briefcase. "Actually, I'm thinking of having you teach me some of the basics so I can help out. If you get requested on an investigative job, then we're not going to be able to get all this search work done. I need to get over my fantasy of being an old-fashioned gumshoe, bite the bullet, and learn how to do your end of the job. It's the part of our business that really seems to be growing."

I waved my boss out the door, sat down, ate my bagel, and got to work. I'd barely gotten into the first file when my phone rang, causing me to practically jump out of my seat. My heart didn't exactly calm down when I heard Detective Desmond Keeler's voice on the other end of the line.

"Mrs. Carrera. I'd like you to come down to the station this morning to answer a few questions."

I knew exactly where he was going with this and sent a silent thank you to Matt for clueing me in.

"What time do you want me there?" I eyed the files spread across my desk with despair, thinking I'd probably be taking them home tonight.

"If you could come down now, I'd appreciate it." On the surface, the words sounded polite and obliging, but I picked up the undercurrent.

Translation: drop everything and get down here before I send a uniform out to pick you up. Detective Keeler was a man who didn't take "no" for an answer, who got what he wanted when he wanted it. He was also a man who stubbornly refused to share even the most innocuous details of a case. I got it. Ongoing investigations and confidentiality. His job and reputation would be on the line if he blabbed all over the place. But it was still frustrating. It made me wonder if the police academy would accept sixty-year-old women, and if so, could I somehow manage to blow through a rookie beat cop assignment and jump straight to detective.

Probably not.

"I'll be right there," I told Keeler. Then I hung up, left J.T. a note, and made a quick attempt to organize the files before heading out.

It was twenty minutes to the Milford Police Station—thirty if traffic was bad, and I drove the whole way with a ghost in my passenger seat, supernaturally flipping through channels to find songs that were meant to convince me that she'd been murdered, and that I needed to help her.

I wasn't convinced it was murder. And I wasn't convinced that I needed to help her. But I *was* worried about how long this ghost was going to be riding around in my car. Would I need to buy a new vehicle to get rid of her? Would she eventually go away? Perhaps if I ripped the stereo out, I could endure her presence in silence.

In Locust Point, bad traffic meant there was paving work dropping the local roads to one-lane alternating, or a line of cars following a combine on a two-lane road with a double yellow and blind curves or trying to get somewhere right after school let out and following a bus for ten minutes. Today there were no impediments as I headed into Milford, and I pulled into the police station a shade less than twenty minutes since I'd left the office, my phone vibrating with a text as I parked the car.

Just got out of a police interrogation with a guy who I'm sure was a mob heavy in a previous life. Was worried waterboarding might be on the agenda. Where are you?

Daisy. I chuckled and texted her back that I was just heading in for some waterboarding of my own, then I left Stacy's ghost in the car and walked toward the door.

Meet me for lunch at Maxine's when you're done. If you're still alive or not behind bars, that is.

Thinking back on those files sitting on my desk, I grimaced and texted Daisy that I'd see her at Maxine's. At this rate, I'd be up all night with the backlog of work I had.

I hurried in, throwing my purse on the conveyer belt for X-ray and passing through the metal detector. Once I was cleared, I headed to the information desk. The man behind the probably bulletproof glass was young and looked as if he'd just stepped out of the shower a scant ten minutes ago. His dark hair was either wet, or heavily gelled, and a waft of aftershave hit my nose through the small slots in the glass. It made me wonder how strong the cologne was without the glass and speculate that his overapplication of man-perfume might have been the reason he'd landed this job away from the other officers.

I introduced myself, telling the young man, who was wearing a tag that said "Snyder," that Detective Keeler had asked me to come in.

He directed me to a bank of hard plastic chairs and asked me to wait. I plopped down, spacing myself evenly between a disheveled woman who appeared to be napping and an older man wearing a suit who couldn't stop tapping his foot against the tile floor.

Despite the implied urgency, Keeler kept me waiting for nearly fifteen minutes. I kept calculating the time in my head, speculating how many files I could still get through before five o'clock. If this interview took an hour, then lunch with Daisy took another hour, and the drive back to the office was twenty to thirty minutes, that would leave me with roughly four hours of work time. Ugh. I could squeeze in a few more hours tonight and maybe come in early tomorrow, but there was no way I could get everything done in time to satisfy our clients' expected turnaround time. J.T. really did need to hire someone else. Or stop with the YouTube videos and take some of the work off my shoulders.

The whole time I mused, the man to my left tapped his food in a persistent rhythm like a background soundtrack to my thoughts.

A woman in uniform opened the door, her hair in a neat bun, her makeup subtle. She smiled at me and I found myself smiling back. If this woman was in on the interrogation, she was well suited to play the nice, supportive, sympathetic good cop foil to Keeler's bad cop personality.

"Mrs. Carrera? Follow me, please."

We wove between a series of metal desks and file cabinets to a door that looked like it might go to a supply closet. When she opened the door, I saw the room held a long table with several chairs instead of shelves full of staples and reams of paper. Seated at one of those chairs was Detective Keeler, a notepad and pen in front of him.

He indicated that I should sit in the chair across from him, rising a few inches from his seat as I approached. It was the only time I'd seen anything close to chivalrous courtesy from him.

"Detective Keeler." I sat in the chair and pulled a notepad and pen of my own from my purse.

A hint of a smile flickered at the corner of his mouth. "Mrs. Carrera. Thank you for coming down. Do you know why I wanted to speak to you?"

"Not really. I'm sure this is about Stacy Mellomaker. I heard on the radio this morning that she'd passed away. Judging from your involvement, I take it her death wasn't due to some sort of early onset heart disease."

"Let's just say there might have been multiple factors involved in Mrs. Mellomaker's passing."

"None of which involve me," I added. Sheesh, between Detective Keeler and the ghost in my car, I felt like I was being maneuvered into investigating a death that in spite of police involvement, I wasn't convinced was a murder.

The detective leaned back in his chair. "You were there at bingo night when she was suddenly taken ill. Tell me what happened. Start from when you first arrived."

"I was running late, so Suzette and Olive grabbed a table for the five of us. When I got there, I grabbed a glass of iced tea, bought my cards, and sat down with the rest of my friends."

Keeler had leaned forward again and was making notes. "Was your friend, Daisy Mercer, there when you arrived?"

I squirmed at the direction his questions were taking. "Yes, as was Kat Lars. All five of us were sitting together for bingo. They'd saved me a seat."

He paused and pulled out a folded piece of paper, pushing it toward me. "Can you note on this table where you and your friends were seated, where Mrs. Mellomaker was, and any other individuals you knew at the bingo game that night?"

I took the paper and began filling it out while he waited patiently. There were quite a few people I hadn't known there that night, and I realized that Daisy had probably done a much better job at this task than I was doing. I noted with question marks next to their names the few people who I wasn't confident about their seating location, then passed it back to the detective.

He spun it around, looked down, then nodded. "You were directly across from Mrs. Mellomaker?"

"Yes. There was someone else sitting in the end chair of that row when I got there, but she left after that first game and moved somewhere else."

"Can you describe her?"

I thought for a second. I'd just arrived and was organizing my things while my friends were busy keeping track of their bingo cards. That was probably the only reason I'd noticed. "Young. Late teens or early twenties? Pretty girl. I'm thinking she might have been mixed race from her skin tone and features. She had straight dark brown hair that was to her shoulders and was wearing a blue t-shirt and jeans with holes in them—you know, the kind you pay extra for."

Keeler looked up at me. "Huh?"

I waved a hand. "You buy them that way. They have holes here and there to look edgy or something."

The detective looked completely perplexed. "Is this a young person thing? Like high school kids?"

"It's a fashion thing. I've seen fifty-year-old women with those jeans on, so it's not just kids."

He nodded and bent to his paperwork. "Anything else you can remember about her?"

"She was thin, but not too thin. Like I said, she was pretty from the quick look I got at her. Not too much makeup. She seemed a bit timid, or nervous, but that could have been because she was moving seats in the middle of a bingo round and didn't want to disturb anyone who was playing."

He glanced up at me again. "She wasn't playing?"

I thought for another second. "I'm not sure. Certainly not that round or she wouldn't have moved in the middle of it. If she gathered up any bingo cards, I didn't notice."

He nodded. "Was there a reason you can think of for why she moved?"

I shrugged. "Stacy was on a winning streak. It was undoubtedly irritating to be sitting next to her. Plus, Stacy practically needed the whole table for the baskets she was winning. The young woman probably couldn't see with them blocking everything."

"But you said she moved after the first game, so there couldn't have been that many baskets on the table?"

I hesitated, embarrassed at my lack of recall. I had been an investigative journalist. I was now a private investigator. I should have better attention to detail than this and getting called on my failings by Keeler was mortifying.

"I think there had been a game or two before I got there because when I arrived Stacy already had one basket on her table. The young woman..." I frowned. "She moved up a few rows. Actually, I do remember! She only had two cards, which is kind of odd because most of the regulars use five or more cards. Stacy had to have thirty spread out in front of her. I don't know how she kept track of them all."

Keeler nodded. "Go on."

"The young woman was talking to the person she'd moved up next to, so maybe she saw a friend and changed seats? I didn't see her talking to Stacy when I'd arrived and was settling in, but it *was* in the middle of a bingo round."

He scribbled a few paragraphs in his notepad before continuing. "Did Mrs. Mellomaker get food or something to drink?"

"Yes. She flagged someone down early on and I think she was asking them to bring her a drink. They brought her a plastic cup. I don't know what was in it, but the VFW served coffee, iced tea, and lemonade that night. For some reason I thought it was coffee."

"Anything after that?"

"When they announced the food was ready, we all headed up. I was behind her in line to grab dinner. She got pot pie and…an iced tea, I think. They served us the pot pie—dished it out right in front of us and handed us a bowl. The drinks we had to pour ourselves from pitchers."

"And you?"

I blinked in surprise. "Pot pie and iced tea. Oh, and I grabbed another bowl for one of my friends that was still playing bingo. Olive and Suzette had stayed behind, while Daisy, Kat, and I had gone up to get food."

His pencil hesitated. "And they were in line with you, right behind Stacy Mellomaker?"

"No, they held back in line a bit. Neither one of them is a fan of Stacy's." I felt bad ratting my friends out like that, but I was pretty sure Detective Keeler already knew this since he'd asked Daisy in for questioning. No doubt, Kat would be next.

"Did they mention what issues they had with Mrs. Mellomaker?"

There was a bit of a nonverbal tussle between me and Detective Keeler, a sort of staring chicken game. I lowered my eyes first, but didn't give in. "Just the usual stuff that would annoy someone. Nothing that was particularly concerning."

There were a few moments of silence, but Detective Keeler must have decided to let that one slide. "Did you see Mrs. Mellomaker eat or drink anything after she'd returned to her seat?"

Here was the direction Matt was afraid the police would take.

"We were playing bingo, so I really wasn't paying much attention. I did see her take a few bites and drink some, but I don't know how much she ate or drank." I went on to tell the detective the rest of the story, from Stacy's walk to the restroom, to Daisy's frantic cry for a 911 call, to the sight of my friend administering CPR.

"Did Daisy Mercer speak with Mrs. Mellomaker that evening? Did she approach the woman or her table?"

I couldn't believe this. Detective Keeler actually thought *Daisy* might have something to do with Stacy's death? "No. Daisy didn't like her. She had good reasons not to like her. But unless you suspect Daisy was jabbing a voodoo doll of Stacy under the table or hexing her from afar, it wasn't her. She was at the table with us from when I arrived, only getting up when we got food and drinks, and even then, she was with Kat the whole time. Whatever happened to Stacy, it wasn't Daisy who did it."

"But what about before you arrived?" Keeler pressed.

I rolled my eyes. "You'll have to ask someone else, but I'm pretty sure Daisy was too busy with getting her bingo cards organized and chatting with our friends to do anything to Stacy. She didn't like the woman, but it wasn't the sort of dislike that makes a person want to kill someone. We were all there to have fun, eat pot pie, and hopefully win at bingo, not murder Stacy Mellomaker."

"But she did win quite a lot of baskets that night," the detective commented.

"What a great motive for murder," I drawled. "Not winning a basket full of cookies really sends a woman over the edge. Whatever happened, Detective Keeler, it wasn't Daisy who did it."

He stared at me, his face impassive. "How long was Daisy

Mercer in the restroom before you heard her cry out for help?"

I scowled, not happy with his dogged fixation on my friend. "Seconds. How did Stacy die, Detective Keeler? I'm guessing you're suspecting poison, but what sort of poison?"

He frowned. "Here's how this goes, Mrs. Carerra. I ask the questions and you answer them."

It was my turn to lean back in my chair. "I'm clearly not a suspect. I didn't know Stacy Mellomaker. I hadn't even heard of her until the bingo game. So, you're not questioning me as a suspect, you're questioning me as a potential witness, as someone who might have valuable information that you need to solve this case. So maybe you should be a bit nicer. And maybe you could share a little bit of information with me so I know what the heck you're looking for."

"I can't share details of the case with you." Keeler glared at me. "You know that. We've been over this before."

"There were nearly fifty people attending that bingo game, and I'm estimating ten to fifteen volunteers working the event. Are you thinking someone roofied her iced tea? Added drugs to the pot pie? Poured antifreeze in her flask?"

Keeler's pencil paused. "She had a flask? Or are you just using that as some sort of metaphor?"

"She had a flask and was taking little secretive drinks out of it all night." I frowned, wondering why it hadn't been in Stacy's purse when the paramedics were going through it for her medicines. I eyed the detective. "You know about the medicines, right? She was on a lot of medicines. Maybe someone switched them out before she even got to the bingo game. Or maybe she had some sort of medical condition and her death was an unfortunate accident. Or maybe one of her medicines reacted adversely with pot pie and iced tea."

There was a buzzing noise. Keeler held up a finger for me to pause as he dug his cell phone out of his pocket and answered. The noise coming from the receiver sounded like the adults in a Peanuts cartoon. The detective made a lot of noncommittal noises, then hung up.

"You can go, Mrs. Carerra. Thank you for coming in."

My mouth dropped open. "What? That's it? No more questions?"

"Nope. Hopefully I won't see you again. Goodbye."

I stood, then hesitated. "Autopsy results?"

A hint of a smile flitted across his face. "Are you joking? You know how long it takes to get autopsy results."

I did. Sometimes preliminary findings were out in five to ten days, but the toxicology reports could take weeks and the DNA tests months. That's what happened when you were a little town in the middle of nowhere.

But if what I thought was true and Gus Mellomaker had enough clout to pressure the Chief of Police to investigate a death that might not even be a murder? He might have enough clout to rush autopsy results.

"Preliminary autopsy results?" I asked. "Her doctor revealed a congenital heart defect that no one knew about? Someone found a suicide note?"

"Let's just say the investigation is on hold unless the M.E. comes back with something surprising. Now get going so I can get back to work on some real cases."

That dratted man wasn't even going to tell me about the autopsy results. A million scenarios filled my imagination. Accidental prescription drug overdose? Interaction of medications and gluten from the pot pie dough squares? With a narrowed glance at Detective Keeler, I got up, headed out of the police station, and walked down to Maxine's to meet Daisy for lunch.

CHAPTER 5

*D*aisy had gotten a head start on lunch. Maxine's didn't serve booze, but my friend had a half-empty milkshake and a plate with a lot of crumbs and three mozzarella sticks on it.

"It's my last supper." She motioned to the plate. "They'll probably be arresting me tonight. Expect to see cop cars outside my house this evening. Think of me at morning yoga and remember that you were always my best friend, Kay."

"Stop. You're not going to get arrested." I sat down across from her and flagged down the waitress, pointing that I wanted a milkshake as well. Daisy's looked seriously good. It might be mid-November, but it was never too cold for a chocolate milkshake.

"They think I did it. Whatever *it* is, anyway. I'm assuming Stacy was poisoned? Although how they can determine that with all the pills she had in her purse, I've got no idea."

"The police jumped the gun. There is no poisoning," I told her, stealing a mozzarella stick. "Whatever they suspected in the beginning, the whole thing is off—or at the very least, on indefinite hold. Keeler got a call while I was in there and he told me he wasn't proceeding unless the M.E. found something unusual in the autopsy."

Daisy slumped in her chair, lifting her hands toward the ceiling. "Thank the Lord and Lady. I seriously thought I was going to end up in jail."

"J.T. would have bailed you out," I told her. "If disliking Stacy Mellomaker was enough motive to be charged with her murder, then half the town would be in jail from what you've told me. When someone young dies suddenly like this, it's human nature to assume foul play—especially if that person wasn't exactly a beloved saint in the community. For all we know, Stacy told her husband about your altercation with her, and he immediately suspected the worst when she was stricken. Clearly the evidence showed otherwise, so celebrate your freedom, and I'll expect you tomorrow morning for yoga."

Daisy stared down at the table. "I wonder what happened to her? When I found her there in the bathroom and started CPR, I knew that she'd been throwing up—and don't ask me how I know that because it's gross. Maybe she was sick and woozy, got lightheaded and fell, hitting her head on the sink as she went down, then asphyxiated on her vomit."

I looked at the remaining two mozzarella sticks, not really wanting to discuss digestive issues during lunch, but just as curious as Daisy about the actual cause of Stacy's death.

"There wasn't any blood or anything to show she hit her head, but the passing out and asphyxiating thing might have happened," I told her. "She was on all those medicines. And I doubt it was milk in her flask."

Daisy tilted her head. "What flask?"

"I saw her drinking out of a flask a couple times that evening. It wasn't in her purse when I went to get it for the EMTs so maybe she had it in her pocket?"

"If so, it would have had to be her coat pocket. She had on yoga pants, remember? Even if she'd had a pair on with pockets, we would have clearly seen the bulge for a flask in them."

I nodded, trying to think back to that evening and remember exactly what had happened. Stacy had been surrounded by all those darned baskets she'd won. With them all over the table and next to her chair, I wouldn't have seen if she'd moved the flask from her purse to her coat pocket, or maybe stuck it in one of the baskets that hadn't been wrapped in cellophane. If I had a flask that I wanted access to without making it obvious I was sneaking drinks of booze, where would I stash it? Where could it be hidden from obvious view, but handy?

"Did you see a flask when we were helping carry her baskets out to put in Kat's car?" I asked. We'd loaded them in before we'd headed off, leaving the others behind to continue with the bingo.

Daisy shook her head. "No, although if I saw one, I might have just thought it was part of the winnings, like the Boozy Broadway basket, or the Wino Wednesday one."

I made a mental note to ask Kat if she'd taken the baskets over to Stacy's yet. I was sure with Stacy in the hospital it hadn't been a huge priority, but I was also sure Kat wouldn't have wanted to be driving around with a dozen baskets in her car, either. If she still had them, I was going to take a quick peek and see if the flask was there.

Not that it mattered. Stacy had clearly died of natural causes, judging from the speed at which Detective Keeler had ousted me from his interview room. There was no sense in wasting my time trying to find a flask with booze in it, espe-cially when I had an ever-growing stack of skip trace files to get through. No one would really care that Stacy was sneaking booze during a bingo game at the VFW, and for all I knew the flask was in her coat pocket. Or someone picked it up off the floor and turned it in to lost and found. It didn't matter.

Except that for some reason, I really wanted to find out what happened to that flask.

Our waitress approached with my milkshake and the pair of us ordered lunch. By the time our sandwiches arrived, Daisy was recovering from her ordeal and we were both on our second milkshakes.

I eyed my pastrami on rye, the plate full of steak-cut fries, the huge milkshake next to the empty one and thought about how I needed to cut this out if I was going to have any hope of fitting into a formal gown next month.

"Daisy? Do I look…" I wasn't sure the correct adjective to use here. "Old" wasn't right. At sixty, I probably seemed ancient to Madison and Henry, but that wasn't the word I was looking for. "Do I look matronly?"

I grimaced, not liking that description, either.

Daisy stopped mid-bite and pulled her sandwich away. "*Matronly?*"

"Well, not really matronly. More like…stodgy. Boring." That wasn't right, either.

Daisy laughed. "Boring women don't get shut in dumpsters while trying to catch a murderer. Boring women don't end up huddled under their desks while the mayor is trying to kill them. Boring women don't wrestle robbers to the floor or go on high-speed chases through the cemetery. No Kay, you most definitely aren't boring. Or stodgy. And you're absolutely not matronly."

I waved my hand. "That's not exactly what I meant. Am I not appealing? You know. Am I past the point where I'd be attractive to someone of the opposite sex?"

Daisy took a bite of her sandwich and chewed thoughtfully. "Matt Poffenberger doesn't think so. He'd jump your bones in a heartbeat."

That was probably true. Even though we'd settled into a just-friends sort of relationship, I knew Matt was attracted to me. It wasn't *Matt* I was feeling somewhat ego-bruised over, though.

"Besides Matt. I never was the sort of woman who would turn heads, even when I was young, but I was pretty. I was smart, bookish, reasonably sophisticated in a career-woman, non-socialite sort of way." Crap. Wasn't that pretty much what Judge Beck had called me? "I know this is weird, and I never thought twice about it until recently, but I feel kind of invisible when it comes to a lot of men. Well, not invisible, but more…matronly and less like a woman someone might actually develop feelings for. Emotional and physical feelings, that is."

Ugh. I should have just kept my mouth shut, eaten my pastrami and fries, and jogged around the block five or six times when I got home tonight to work it all off.

"So, Judge Beck then." Daisy tried but didn't quite manage to hide a grin behind a swipe of her napkin.

I felt my face burn. "No! I mean, sort of. It's not like I want him to…. It's just the other night…and I got to thinking and felt…." Sheesh, this was all so embarrassing.

"Spill it, Kay," Daisy commanded. "What happened with you and your good-looking but very intimidating roomie the other night? Is this something we need to discuss in private? Did he kiss you?"

"No!" I squealed, then clamped my hand over my mouth and looked around. Thankfully none of the other customers seemed to have noticed my outburst. "It was all completely proper, Daisy."

"Of course. This is Judge Beck we're talking about here. I think proper is his middle name." Daisy rolled her eyes.

"He most definitely did not kiss me." And now the image of that very thing was stuck in my head, making me feel flustered and tingly—and guilty. *I'm so sorry, Eli. I love you. I miss you. And I shouldn't be thinking these things when it's not even a year after your death.*

"Well, that's a darned shame because he should," Daisy told me. I wasn't sure if she was teasing or not. Knowing my friend, probably not. "So, what *did* happen the other night?"

"He asked me to go with him to a work function. It's a swanky Christmas party that some hot-shot law firm puts on in the capitol. There will be a lot of movers and shakers there and he needs to go and rub elbows with people."

Daisy ate a fry. "He's gonna kiss you."

"No, he's not," I shot back. "Eli used to have to go to some of these things. It's not romantic. He needs someone to accompany him, but obviously he can't go with Heather, and Madison is too young to be his plus one. I'm smart and know my way around backstabbing professional people, so he asked me."

"Riiiiight." Daisy ate another fry and speared me with a perceptive look.

"Seriously. He just needs someone to go with who he knows won't embarrass him."

"Kay, you're such an idiot sometimes—and I mean that with all the love in the world. There's no reason why he can't go to this thing alone. He asked you because he wants to be with *you*. This is a date, only he's got all sorts of excuses about why this isn't a date because he's Mister Proper, and proper men don't date when they're still not technically divorced and the woman they would love to haul off to bed is a recent widow."

It felt like my face was on fire. I looked around again to make sure no one was staring at us or listening in on this absolutely mortifying conversation.

"He *could* go to this thing alone, but it wouldn't be ideal. Trust me, I went to a ton of these events with Eli back before the accident. It's awkward to show up alone. There would be talk about the divorce, and all the bored wives would be wondering if he was interested in an affair. The only thing worse would be if he showed up with some twenty-year-old supermodel. It's not a date. He asked me because I won't embarrass him, and it would be clear to everyone in the room that I'm not someone he cheated on Heather with, or that I'm even a current fling. People will probably think I'm his older sister or something. He asked me because I'm not the sort of woman anyone would assume he was doing anything scandalous with."

Daisy's expression changed. Instead of the teasing look, I got a warm, sympathetic glance. "It's okay, you know. You can feel something for another man and not be betraying your marriage vows or Eli's memory. Being attracted to Judge Beck, or anyone, isn't wrong, Kay. It's just human."

I blinked back sudden tears. "We're just friends. And it doesn't matter what I think or feel, because he'd never see me as anything more than a friend—an older friend who is smart, reasonably sophisticated and won't embarrass him at a party that's very important for his career."

Daisy reached out and took my hand, giving it a quick squeeze. "Hon, trust me on this one. Judge Beck sees a whole lot more in you than a smart, sophisticated, older friend, but he's not going to make even a hint of a move until the ink is dry on his divorce papers and he's sure you're not rebounding from the loss of your beloved husband of thirty-five years."

My mouth wobbled as I smiled. "Thirty-seven years. And I think you're wrong."

"Either way, you're going to knock his proper socks off at this party, even if I have to rob a bank to pay for it all," Daisy announced as she pulled her hand away and scooped up her sandwich. "Dress. Hair. Makeup. We're putting Cinderella to shame. Text me the date of this shindig, and I'll set it all up."

I laughed, shaking my head. "I've got a bunch of dresses upstairs from when Eli and I were going to formal parties. And I can do my own hair and makeup. There's no need to spend a lot of money neither of us have when all I need to do is look presentable and smart."

"Oh, hon, you are going to look so much more than presentable and smart. Silver fox isn't just a label for men, you know. We're going to make you a silver vixen. Powerful. Smart. Sexy. Trust me, I've got this covered."

I knew better than to argue with Daisy when she was on a roll like this, so I ate my fries and resigned myself to a lot of shopping trips and a day at the spa next month. She'd make it all fun—probably more fun than the actual party itself.

I was blessed to have a friend like Daisy in my life. Truly blessed.

CHAPTER 6

I was making some serious inroads into the stack of skip trace files and humming "Poison" by Alice Cooper, which Stacy's ghost had insisted on playing as we'd driven back from Milford, when a woman walked through the door. She looked to be in her early thirties, well-dressed with tweed wool coat, leather gloves, and a scarf that might have been Burberry or might have been a reasonably priced knock-off.

"Can I help you?" I gave the woman my friendly-but-professional smile because one never knew the circumstances that led someone to visit our offices. She could need to make bail for a wayward brother. She could be looking to hire us to confirm suspicions of a straying spouse. She could want us to track down that guy who wrote her a bad check at last month's Apple Harvest Craft Festival.

"I'm looking to hire an investigator. Are you Kay Carrera?" She smiled, and I saw that it took some effort. I also saw the red puffy eyelids and blotchy face she'd tried to conceal with carefully applied makeup.

"Yes, I am." I stood and pulled a chair over to my desk.

"Here. Sit and let me get you some coffee while you tell me what you need an investigator for."

She sat and promptly burst into tears, causing me to scramble around for a box of tissues.

After a few seconds, she'd managed to wrestle her emotions back under control. The woman carefully blotted under her eyes, sniffed, then took a breath. "My sister died. Someone killed her and the police won't do anything about it. I want to hire you to find out who murdered her. I saw the YouTube videos. You've caught murderers before. If anyone can find Stacy's killer, I know you can."

Even before she'd mentioned Stacy's name, I knew who she was talking about. The past year aside, we didn't usually have a lot of murders in our county, nor the sort of deaths that might lead a sibling to suspect foul play.

"You're her sister?" I waited for her nod, for her to introduce herself as Brenda Gris in a shaky voice before I proceeded to ask her why she thought her sister was murdered.

"She was thirty-five. Healthy, fit thirty-five-year-old women don't drop dead of a heart attack." Brenda lifted her hands and shook her head at the improbability of such a thing. "And they don't collapse in a bathroom at the VFW, either."

I'm sure they did, although I was equally sure it wasn't a common occurrence, but I understood where Brenda was going with this. I also thought grief was clouding her judgement and convincing her to see foul play where there was none. I loved the idea of getting away from these skip trace files for a bit of real detective work, and I also had questions about how Stacy Mellomaker had died, but I didn't want to waste someone's money on what might be a grief-fueled snipe hunt.

Then I thought of the ghost in the passenger seat of my

car, of all the songs she'd been playing for me. Of the Huey Lewis song "Doing It All for My Baby." She'd had a four-year-old daughter. A sister. Maybe I owed it to this woman to listen to what she had to say, no matter what my personal feelings were on the matter.

"What did the doctors at the hospital say about her death?" I asked as gently as I could.

Brenda pulled a stack of files out of her tote bag and passed them over to me. "Here. I got copies of everything. She had me listed as having medical power of attorney because she didn't trust Gus, so I was able to get access to everything. I don't understand it all, but they told me they thought she'd taken too many of one of her medications as well as other medications that she was no longer supposed to be using and maybe had a bit of food poisoning as well. At first, they were asking me about suicide, but I told them that was impossible, so then they said she accidently overdosed on her medicines."

I had winced at the food poisoning comment, hoping that if I took this case, it didn't end up leading me to a conclusion that would hurt Matt or the VFW. "There *were* a lot of medicines in Stacy's purse when she collapsed. Did the doctors say it was those medicines that caused the problem, or other ones?"

Brenda's laugh held a note of bitterness. "I'm assuming whatever lab reports they ran are in there. Not that I can read them. I included a list of all the medicines Stacy was on, as well as ones she had on hand that she might or might not have been taking. My sister had some hypochondriac tendencies, but despite her mental health issues and a few minor health concerns, she was physically in perfect condition."

"The one medicine was for acid reflux," I commented.

"And another was a controlled substance—a prescription pain reliever. And another was a sedative."

Brenda sighed. "Nexium. She also had both Xanax and Ambien because she had insomnia and panic attacks as well as stomach issues from anxiety. She'd been prescribed Adderall because she was sure she had ADHD a few years back. Then there was the bipolar medication and something for intestinal problems. She hurt her back lifting weights a few years ago and had a prescription for pain relievers. The list goes on and on, and she never threw any leftover medicines away, just in case she might need them. Every little twinge, and Stacy was sure she was dying. That's the way she was even when she was a child."

"It sounds quite possible she might have inadvertently taken some pills that shouldn't have been taken together." I was trying to be as circumspect as possible, but just listening to the list of medicines made me agree with the doctors.

"Stacy was smart. She wasn't the bimbo, gym-rat, trophy wife some people made her out to be. She was wicked smart and knew her medicines. Just because she was paranoid about having some rare disease didn't mean she didn't carefully read and study side effects and interactions for what she was prescribed. It drove us all nuts." Brenda took a deep breath. "We fought. We fought constantly. There was a lot about her lifestyle that I didn't agree with, and her behavior that I didn't like. There were times when I wished she wasn't my sister, but I still loved her. I'm three years younger. Growing up, we were the only friends each other had. As much as we fought, she's still my sister and I can't let her murder go without making every attempt toward justice."

I'd never had a sibling, but I understood. Even if my investigation turned up nothing, this woman would rest easier knowing that she'd made sure her sister wasn't murdered. I wasn't sure if the ghost in my car would ever accept "accident" or "natural causes," but I got the feeling Brenda would as long as I'd explored all the possibilities. It would be up to me to be thorough and do that without unduly wasting both her money and my time.

"So, what exactly *was* Stacy on the night she collapsed?" I asked.

Brenda shrugged. "According to her primary care doctor, she was supposed to be only on the Nexium and the occasional Xanax. I'm sure she was taking Ambien because she regularly relied on that to get to sleep at night. I've never known her to take it during the day, though."

"And the pain medication? The Oxycodone?"

"As far as I know, no. That back thing had cleared up long ago, and she made no mention to me of anything she'd need to take prescription pain relief for."

"She wasn't taking the psychiatric medications, then?" I asked.

Brenda shook her head. "I'm pretty sure she wasn't. Stacy was diagnosed when she was still in college but had never found any medication that really worked for her. She often went long spells without any pharmacological treatment but had just started with a new psychiatrist. I had lunch with her a few weeks ago and she was complaining about him and what he'd put her on. She didn't like the side effects and said she'd stopped taking them after a few weeks."

"Why would she carry around all of those medicines if she wasn't taking them?" I countered, thinking that Stacy may have hid the extent of her drug use from her sister.

"Stacy was one of those people who liked to have everything handy, just in case. She was worried that she'd be out somewhere and have an issue with her stomach, or her back would twinge, or she'd start to have a panic attack. My sister didn't want anyone to see her vulnerable. She had to always be perfect, composed, at the top of her game. She had to always be the winner, and even if she was in pain or sick, she'd never want anyone to know it. I'm sure most of those pills in her purse she hadn't taken in months or even years."

I eyed the woman skeptically and she pointed at the folder on my desk.

"I'm not sure exactly what they found in her lab work, but the doctor told me it was mostly a sedative and some alcohol. Like I said, at first they thought suicide, but I told them no one attempts suicide in the middle of a bingo game, especially Stacy. If she'd wanted to kill herself, and she didn't, she would have done it at home."

"Where no one could intervene until it was too late," I mused, thinking that even at the VFW, the intervention had been too late.

"No, where no one would be gaping at her convulsing or bleeding, lying on a dirty bathroom floor. Stacy was incredibly concerned about her image. She needed people to respect her, even fear her. She would have never done this to herself, never allowed herself to look weak like that in front of a bunch of people. I told the doctor there was no way it was suicide, and that Stacy wouldn't have taken the risk of downing all that stuff in a public place."

"Where was her husband when all this at the hospital was going on?" It seemed odd that Stacy had given her sister medical power of attorney, and even more strange that the woman's husband hadn't asserted himself in medical decisions regarding his own wife.

Brenda fought to keep the anger from her face and failed. "He doesn't care. I'll admit that Stacy married him for his money, and that she wasn't exactly faithful, but she was still his wife and the mother of his child. He showed up at the hospital and that's about it. The guy was ready to sign off on suicide, donate her organs, and get her in the ground as soon as possible."

"Would *he* have wanted her dead?" I mused. Clearly not for insurance purposes or he would have fought the notion of suicide. Perhaps he was angry at Stacy's infidelity, or that his trophy wife hadn't turned out as he'd hoped. I was sure a man that rich would have had the sense to get a prenuptial agreement. Divorce would have hit Stacy far more than it would her husband. Most likely she would have left with some small sum and child support, losing all of her social status in the process.

Was that it? Had Gus Mellomaker found another trophy wife to take Stacy's place, and Stacy was going to make waves during the divorce? If she'd contested, it would have dragged out for possibly three years which was a long time for an elderly man who might want a new shiny woman on his arm before he died.

Brenda hesitated. "Yesterday I would have said yes to that. Now… I think he's relieved that she's gone and out of his life without him having to deal with lawyers and an ugly divorce proceeding, but I'm not sure if that would be enough for Gus to kill her over. That's what I want you to find out, though. Did Gus kill her? Did someone else? She wasn't beloved in the community—I'm sure you know that."

I did. "So how did the police get involved in this? If her husband was ready to call it suicide and the doctors agreed, then why was there a detective on this case not four hours ago?"

"That was me." Brenda blew out a puff of air. "I had medical power of attorney. I insisted it wasn't an accidental overdose or suicide, so the doctors said they'd send samples away for a more detailed look into the lab results and send her body to the M.E. for a formal ruling. I think they did that more to get me off their back— to lob the whole thing over to someone else."

"But there was a detective assigned to the case," I pressed.

"Why waste departmental resources on that? I mean, I get that they'd consider it a potential homicide until the M.E. ruling came in, but to actively work a case before the cause of death wasn't even decided? It seems odd."

Her smile was a bit sheepish. "That was me again. I insisted that Gus call the Chief of Police. They go way back, and the chief agreed to have one of his detectives look into it."

I was beginning to believe that Brenda had more in common with her sister than I'd originally thought. Maybe she was more personable, but both women pushed and pushed until they got their way, not taking "no" for an answer.

"Okay, so the police got involved, but now something happened and the investigation's off or on hold," I told her.

She nodded. "The police told me they'd spoken to the doctors from the hospital and that there was nothing more they could do unless the lab results from the medical examiner came back with something really unexpected. That's when I decided I needed to hire someone. This wasn't suicide. It wasn't an accident. She was murdered."

I disagreed, but a client was a client. Explaining our rates, I pulled a standard contract form out of the drawer on my desk. Then I warned Brenda that I might find nothing at all, or that my findings might corroborate what the doctors at the hospital had determined.

"I might also dig up a whole lot of unpleasant information about your sister that retroactively you'll wish you would have not known," I added.

She laughed. "Stacy wasn't a saint. I doubt there's anything you could find out that would shock me. How much of a retainer do you need?"

"Think about the limit of what you want to spend," I told her. "You can always raise it if you want to keep going. I'll give you regular reports, but I don't want you thinking that two thousand dollars is going to reveal your sister's murderer. I might dig for weeks and still find nothing definitive."

She nodded. "I'm not rich, and I'm pretty sure Stacy left everything to Sheyanne—what little she had, that is. Gus kept her on a pretty tight leash financially."

I took the contract from her and the check, then got down to business. "Why did her husband restrict her finances? Had she been careless with money in the past? Was there a lot of friction in their relationship?"

"There wasn't a whole lot of anything in their relationship," Brenda drawled. "Maybe in the beginning, but since Sheyanne was born, Gus and Stacy were distant at best. Her bedroom was at the opposite side of the house. They rarely saw each other. Stacy had never had access to Gus' money, though. When they were married, he set her up with an account and put regular monthly deposits into it. I know this because she complained all the time about how she had to go asking him for more money for clothing, or club memberships, or general expenses."

I pulled over a pad of paper and made a note. "Did they argue over money?"

"I don't think it was so much arguing as that Stacy hated to feel like she was begging. Status was important to her. I think Gus was okay with allowing her extra for organizing social functions or things like that, but she had to go to him each month and make a case for it, and she hated that. Her car, anything major was in his name, too."

"What about their daughter? Did Gus handle expenses related to her, or did Stacy?"

"After Sheyanne was born, Stacy did get an additional sum of money, but Gus handled things like the nanny, and private preschool. I remember Stacy telling me if she needed extra money for clothes or a fitness class she wanted to take, the easiest way was to tell Gus it was for Sheyanne and to make it seem like he was depriving his daughter by not upping Stacy's monthly allowance."

This couple seemed more divorced than married. It was almost as though Stacy had been getting alimony and child support and not truly sharing in her husband's income. But I guess when a man married a woman roughly fifty years his junior, he was bound to be cautious about her motives.

The whole thing seemed sordid and ugly. Why couldn't people just marry for love?

"Do you think Gus had motive to want Stacy dead?" I asked.

Brenda wrinkled her nose in thought. "I'll admit with his I-don't-care attitude at the hospital, I did think that. I don't know. Stacy would have gotten nothing if she'd left. Maybe she'd have gotten some child support for Sheyanne, but I'm pretty sure Gus would have fought her on custody."

"He wouldn't have been jealous over a lover, or felt it was a blow to his ego if Stacy was seeing someone else, or even thinking of leaving him?"

She shook her head. "Gus was controlling financially, but that was it. I got the impression that he didn't care if Stacy screwed around, and that he would have been thrilled if she left. Yes, she had lovers, but she was reasonably discreet about it. She was concerned enough about her reputation in certain social circles that she wasn't flaunting lovers around town, making out with them in public, or anything like that."

I tapped my pencil on my lip. "Maybe Gus wanted her to leave, and she wouldn't go? Maybe he wanted a divorce and she was digging in her heels?"

"I got the impression from Stacy that the prenup was iron-clad no matter who initiated the divorce. All Gus had to do was file and have all her stuff moved to an apartment across town. I don't know why he didn't do that because he clearly didn't want to stay married to her. Maybe because of Sheyanne. Maybe because of apathy. I don't know."

I frowned and wrote a question mark on my notepad, thinking that Stacy's husband might have had a secret no one knew about.

"Would Gus be open to me talking to him about this?" I asked.

"Probably. In the hospital I told him if he didn't call the police and get them to investigate, that I was going to hire someone on my own, so he can't be surprised if you show up on his doorstep. He'll probably talk to you rather than have me pestering the heck out of him about it if he says 'no.'" She laughed. "That's how Stacy got things done with him. Annoy Gus enough and he usually gives in. The woman had a new car every two years and a wardrobe that an A-list celebrity would envy, but having to go to him all the time made her feel like a pauper."

I put another question mark next to Gus' name, thinking there wasn't a lot of motive there for murder. But over-whelmingly it seemed in these cases the killer tended to be the spouse, so it was worth checking out.

The spouse or the lover.

"Do you know who Stacy was currently sleeping with? And if there were any past relationships that hadn't ended on good terms?"

"I do know that she had a casual thing with Dennis Moore years ago. He's a tax attorney in Milford. He's married and from what I understood, it was just physical. They'd meet a few times a week, do the deed, then go on about their day. That ended around the time Stacy got preg-nant with Sheyanne."

I paused in my notes, looking up at Brenda with raised eyebrows.

"Yes, I always wondered if Gus really was Sheyanne's father. No, I didn't ask. I'm sure Stacy might have had the occasional one-night stand with someone besides Dennis, and I've got no idea if her marriage with Gus still included sex at that point or not."

I grimaced and made another note, worried that any investigation might uncover something about that little girl's parentage. I really didn't care about digging up dirt on Stacy Mellomaker, but I hated to see an innocent four-year-old suffer because of a secret that would be better off buried.

"So, Dennis Moore? How did Dennis take the breakup? And was there anyone else? I'd heard rumors about someone at the health club?"

"I don't think Dennis cared one way or another about their breakup. I'm not even sure he didn't initiate it. Stacy didn't seem upset, but she didn't complain about Dennis calling her or begging her to come back or being angry at all. I think it was just another business arrangement that had run its course as far as the pair of them were concerned."

I made another note, liking Stacy Mellomaker even less than I had earlier today. A gold-digger. Cheating on her husband with what sounded like unemotional, transactional sex. Was there anything redeeming about this woman?

"As for the personal trainer at the gym," Brenda continued. "I'm pretty sure he and Stacy had a steady thing for some years, although I'm not positive. She never told me definitively about anyone besides Dennis, and I found out about that after it was long over."

"Anyone else she might have been seeing?"

She nodded. "I do know there was a man she'd fallen for —someone she only met recently. I'd never seen her quite this crazy about someone before. I don't know who he was— she was very cagey about it, saying there would be trouble if it got out, so I think he might have been married. She'd changed the last few weeks, and I could tell she was head-over-heels for this guy."

"Enough to leave Gus?" I asked.

Brenda thought for a moment. "I doubt it. Stacy liked the money too much. Being broke, having to get a job, and living with someone who would probably be going through a really expensive divorce… No, Stacy was a realist. She may have loved this guy more than she'd loved any other man in her life, but I doubt that would have been enough for her to leave Gus' money behind."

I frowned down at my notepad. "One more thing: If Gus were to have died before Stacy, would she have inherited anything?"

She shot me a quizzical look. "I'm sure Sheyanne has a trust fund or something, so Stacy would have been able to get support money from that while her daughter was a minor, and I believe state law prohibits a married couple from completely disowning the other, so I'm sure she would have gotten something if Gus had died first. I just don't know what. As savvy as Gus is about money, I'd bet it's all tied up in trusts, and the actual remaining estate would have been so small that Stacy wouldn't have gotten much. But I don't really know."

I hadn't been sure why I'd asked that question, given that it was Stacy who was dead and not her elderly husband, but for some reason I was curious. Jealousy, revenge, and money seemed to be the big motivators when it came to murder, and I was just trying to cover all my bases.

Pushing my notepad aside, I escorted Brenda to the door, then glanced back at the stack of skip trace files beside my computer. These needed to be done, but there was a contract and a check on my desk and a client that needed answers. I'd leave J.T. a note along with the paperwork and check from Brenda, load all these files into my briefcase, and see how much I could get done in what remained of the day. The skip trace files might need to wait until tonight after dinner, because I had a few people I needed to see.

And a ghost in the passenger seat of my car who it seemed was going to get what she wanted in death just as she had in life.

As it turned out, I ended up staying in the office until five o'clock working on skip traces. Calling the number Brenda had provided led me straight to Gus Mellomaker's message service. It took me all of three minutes to find Dennis Moore's office number, and that also ended with asking for a return call. I did get through to Fitness Forever and made an appointment for tomorrow afternoon for a tour for potential membership and personal training. I typed in the social security number and date of birth that Brenda had given me and printed out everything I could find on Stacy Harris Mellomaker, stuffing the paperwork into a folder to take home. By the time J.T. came back to the office, I'd made appointments to meet with Dennis Moore and Gus Mellomaker and was digging into the third skip trace.

J.T. looked at the check from Brenda, then at the skip trace files, then back at the check. "What can I do to help?"

"Clone me?" I threw up my hands in exasperation. "Can we get an extension on some of these skip traces? I don't have the time to train you to do them." I knew the answer was to have him investigate the Mellomaker case, but Brenda had asked for me. And I was itching to do something besides sit in a chair in front of a computer.

"I hate to miss our deadline on these. Credicorp has sent a lot of business our way the last few months. I don't want them thinking they need to shop around for another firm. Can you work overtime?"

"Do I get *paid* overtime?" J.T. was cheap, and I'd brought work home many nights in the past without getting any extra compensation for it. It was time I put my foot down and started insisting he pay me for the extra work.

"Straight time, but not more than an additional two hours per night."

I took a breath, straightened my spine and looked my boss straight in the eyes. "The company gets paid per skip trace, which means *you* get paid per skip trace. It's not like I'm slacking and working slow. The workload has increased, but my hours have still remained the same. Which means I'm making less per hour of work, while you're making more. That's not fair, J.T. Plus, you're holding a check from a client in your hand—a client that you'll charge more than double my hourly rate. You want me to meet the deadline on these skip traces? Fine. I'll make that happen even if I have to work evenings this week. *And* I'll do the work on this investigation. But I'm not doing all that for an extra two hours of straight time. You need to trust me not to rip you off and pay me what's fair for my work."

He held up a hand—the one holding the check. "Okay, you're right. Time and a half for overtime. Just don't bankrupt me, Kay."

I rolled my eyes. "Not likely, *Gator* Pierson. Now go cash that and let me get back to work."

J.T. headed out and I managed to get a few more of the skip traces done before bundling up all the files and heading for home. It was going to be a rough evening. I was starting to feel guilty about all this work. Between Judge Beck and I, the kids were lucky to get a microwaved dinner lately, and the pair of us were often working long into the night. We needed a vacation. Well, he and the kids needed a vacation, and I needed a week where I could just lay around my house and pet my cat, knit, read, and bake cookies.

That would be the life. Well, until I got bored which would probably happen after two or three days, then I'd be begging for all these skip trace files.

I pulled into the driveway after an annoying ride home. Stacy Mellomaker's ghost wouldn't budge from my passenger seat, and she insisted on subjecting me to her musical choices. Luckily the ride wasn't too long, and I'd only had to hear Tom Jones' "Delilah," which was actually quite catchy, and Robbie Fulks' upbeat country song, "She Took a Lot of Pills and Died," which seemed surprisingly on point.

I was just getting out of my car when I looked over to see my neighbor's car coming down the street. Kat, no doubt just getting home from work herself. I waited while she parked and got out before calling her name, waving, and jogging across the street and down the sidewalk to her house. Kat stood patiently by her car, a briefcase in one hand and a huge leather purse in the other.

"Did you drop those baskets off for Stacy Mellomaker yet?" I asked, somewhat out of breath from my short run. I really did need to start doing more than just yoga.

Kat shook her head. "No. I sent her an e-mail and was going to wait until she was out of the hospital, but then I heard the news. I can't believe she's actually gone. I mean, she was so young. And now I'm not sure what I'm supposed to do with these things. Does her husband want them? Her sister? I doubt it would be courteous to call the day after someone died and ask who gets their bingo winnings, but if I wait too long those cookies are going to be stale or moldy."

"I'll run them over," I offered. "I'm headed over there in the morning anyway. We can go ahead and load them in my car and I'll just drop them off."

"I thought you didn't know Stacy Mellomaker." Kat shot me a curious look. "Do you know her husband? Is this a condolence call? Ooh, or are you on a case? Kay, are you investigating Stacy's death?"

Gossip spread in this town like a brush fire in August, and I didn't want either my client's confidentiality to be breached or the word to get out before I could question everyone I needed to question.

"My husband knew Gus Mellomaker years ago. It's been a while, but I feel obliged to at least visit and pay my respects." It was a lie, but a believable one. My husband had been well known in Locust Point, and we had moved in a lot of different social circles prior to his accident. For all I knew, he'd had a few business lunches with Gus a few decades ago.

"Oh, I'm so sorry." Kat looked over toward her front door. "I really *would* appreciate it if you took them over. I've got them on the dining room table, and Will keeps eyeing the one with the cookies in it. I'm worried that if they're still in my house come tomorrow, that basket's going to be missing."

I chuckled, knowing what she meant. Daisy had really wanted that basket, too. "Why don't I bring my car on down and we can go ahead and load them up? That way we don't have to do it first thing tomorrow morning, and Will won't be tempted any longer."

"That would be great." She held up her briefcase and her purse. "I'm going to take these inside. Come on in once you park your car."

I headed back home at a more leisurely pace, started up my car, and drove it the short distance to the Larses' home.

Kat and Will's house was immaculate and charmingly decorated, just as gorgeous inside as it was outside. The furniture was a tasteful blend of antiques and comfortable contemporary, all accented by Kat's beautiful hand-knit lace. In most homes, the lace would have made the house feel as if it belonged to a stern grandmother who covered her sofas with plastic and wouldn't let you eat the mints from the cut-glass candy dish on the coffee table, but here they lent a warm, cozy, elegant note to the rooms. Kat popped her head out of the kitchen when she heard the door, then came fully into view carrying two glasses of wine.

"Sit. Have some wine. I'm always over on your porch drinking. It's about time I got to play hostess."

"I would have thought you'd be fed up playing hostess," I teased as I took one of the glasses and lowered myself onto a velvet upholstered sofa. Kat and Will ran a bed and breakfast out of their home. It was supposed to be Will's business—one he'd put together after being laid off at his job—but Kat ended up doing most of the cooking and behind-the-scenes work. It had been a source of tension between the two, since Kat was still holding down a nine-to-five job. Actually, quite a few things had been a source of tension between the two, although their marriage seemed to be more solid in the last few months then it had been over the summer.

"Things have gotten better," she admitted with a smile. "We had quite a few bookings this fall and are looking at a full house all through December. It was enough to convince Will to hire a housekeeping service to take care of linens and room cleaning for changeovers. He does the rooms in the mornings, and I do turn-downs, so it's not as much work for me as before. He also signed up for some cooking classes at the community college, so I'm not constantly late for work getting breakfast together for the guests."

"I'm so glad," I told her. "And I'm happy his business is turning a profit."

"Me, too. That lay off was such a blow to him. Will hates feeling like he's not contributing and hates not feeling productive. I had my doubts about turning our home into an inn, but he's worked really hard at it and I'm proud of him."

"You've worked hard, too." I toasted her with my wine. "I know it wasn't easy working all day, then coming home and having to wash sheets and clean bathrooms."

She nodded. "Will does the website and the marketing. He's the one who ran Facebook ads and got brochures printed up to hand out at that wedding expo. I cleaned and made omelets, but he's the one who has made sure we had paying guests."

"Well, I'm excited for your success." We chatted for a bit about holiday decorations, recipes for cookies, and the progress that the younger Mr. Peter was making on cleaning up the house next door. After we'd finished our wine, Kat took me into the dining room where once again I was struck by the number of baskets Stacy Mellomaker had won at bingo the other night. I swear, it seemed as if they'd multiplied in the last two days.

"You sure you don't mind taking these over?" Kat asked as she picked up one of the baskets.

"Are you eyeing the cooking basket as well?" I teased.

She laughed. "No. I just feel bad about saddling you with this when I was the one who said I'd do it. I just don't know what to say to them, you know? I really didn't like Stacy all that much, although her sister is nice."

I grabbed a basket and followed Kat to the door, trying to figure out how to word my questions without arousing suspicion. "Stacy and her sister are really that different?"

"Very different. For all her volunteer work, Stacy wasn't all that much on charity or serving others. It all seemed more like a ploy to make herself look good, to position herself in Milford high society—whatever high society Milford has, anyway. It was never about the new roof on the church, or the children's wing on the library; it was always about her own ego. Brenda isn't on as many committees, probably because she didn't marry an old wealthy guy and has to work like the rest of us, but she seems more earnest. She seems more like she's invested in whatever the project or cause is. She listens to other people's opinions and builds consensus where Stacy would bulldoze over everyone to get her way."

I opened the back door to my car and slid the basket in, waiting while Kat did the same. "I guess two pushy, argumentative people in one family would have made for a horrible childhood," I mused. "One has to give in just to keep the peace."

"Oh, don't get me wrong. Brenda is just as pushy," Kat said as we headed in to grab more of the baskets. "Brenda just does it with a smile. She wears you down until you finally see things her way, where Stacy didn't really care about getting your agreement. And Brenda can be persuaded to change her mind, where Stacy would dig in and double down even if she was clearly wrong."

"Doesn't seem like the best method for ingratiating yourself into Milford high society," I commented, grabbing another basket.

"Stacy felt there was no problem in life she couldn't solve, no door she couldn't open with money and persistence." Kat shook her head. "But I shouldn't speak ill of the dead like this. I'm sure she had people who loved her—her husband, her daughter, her sister. I'm sorry for their loss."

I kept my mouth shut, thinking that out of the three, the daughter and sister were the only ones who would be mourning Stacy Mellomaker's death. And that was sad.

We finished loading the baskets, and I drove the short

distance to my home. I let out my cat, carried all the baskets into the house and set aside the ones where the cellophane covering had clearly not been disturbed. Three of the twelve baskets didn't have any covering on them, and two looked as if they'd been opened and re-tied.

"What are you doing?" Henry peeked his head around the corner of the room.

"Looking for something." I sighed as I sorted through the contents of the Cocoa Lovers basket.

"Does that one have cookies in it?" he asked, coming into the room.

"Yes, and no, you can't have any. These aren't my baskets. Another lady won them at bingo the other night, and I'm dropping them off tomorrow on my way in to work."

He eyed me with raised eyebrows. "Why are you going through them if they belong to someone else? Did something accidently get put in a basket that shouldn't have been there?"

This boy was far too smart. He reminded me a lot of his father. "Someone might have dropped something in one of the baskets, and I'm checking to see."

"Can I help?"

I hesitated, not wanting to tell Henry that I was looking for a flask, nor wanting to explain what a flask was or the circumstances around why I was looking for it. "I think I can manage on my own, although I would appreciate some help loading these all back into my car in a bit."

He nodded, then turned to leave, casting one last longing glance at the cookie basket.

"I'll bake some this weekend," I promised him.

"The peanut butter ones with the chocolate kisses on top?" he asked.

"If that's what you want, then yes. I'll even make extra so

you and Madison can take some back to your mother's house Sunday night."

"Awesome." He grinned and headed out of the room. I heard his footsteps on the stairs as I was going through the Terrific Teas basket and wondered if he was still doing his homework or was off to play a video game. Peanut butter with chocolate kisses. All the gourmet cookies I made, and his favorite was one of the most simplistic ones. They *were* good, though—especially when the kisses were all soft and melty from the warm cookies, and the whole thing dissolved in your mouth in a gooey chocolate and crumbly peanut butter mess.

I examined all the baskets, peering through the cellophane at the ones that hadn't been opened and still didn't see the flask. It probably didn't matter. With all the pills Stacy had been taking, I doubted that a few sips of alcohol did much to contribute to her death. The more I thought about it, the guiltier I felt about taking the case. I was wasting Brenda's money. Yes, I wanted Stacy's ghost gone from my car, but unlike the spirit and her sister, I really believed Stacy's death was from accidental overdose and not due to anything nefarious. I guess peace of mind was worth two thousand dollars to Brenda, though. I'd do my best, try to keep costs down, and hopefully in a few days have enough evidence to prove to Brenda that no one had murdered her sister.

Maybe then I could drive my car in peace and be able to choose what I listened to on the radio.

There was no flask, but what I did find in one of the baskets was a one-month trial membership for Fitness Forever. Feeling somewhat guilty, I slid the card into my purse and rearranged the basket contents to cover up for my theft. That place was ridiculously expensive, and my tour tomorrow would only allow me a brief glimpse at the gym where Stacy Mellomaker seemed to have spent the majority of her day. If there were shady circumstances around her death, then I might need more access to the club then a five-minute tour.

Yes, I stole it, but I doubted Stacy's husband was going to use a certificate for a women's-only health club, and her daughter was too young to take advantage of the offer. I reconciled my lapse in ethics by silently promising that if the case was solved before the trial membership expired, I'd discontinue use of the club. And I'd only go as part of my investigative duties, not because I wanted to take that high-powered spin class that Kat had told me about, or join Daisy's yoga session, or swim laps in the heated indoor pool.

"Pizza will be here in five minutes at most." Judge Beck leaned around the dining room entrance. "The kids are swamped with homework. I'm swamped with homework. You look like you're swamped with…whatever all that is."

I waved a hand at the baskets. "They're Stacy Mellomaker's winnings from bingo. I'm going to see her husband tomorrow morning and told Kat I'd take them over."

Judge Beck entered the room and picked up the Backyard Barbeque basket. "Were you and your husband friends with Gus? I assumed from our conversation last night that you didn't know either of them."

"I don't." I hesitated, but then decided that Judge Beck was hardly going to be gossiping about my case. "Her sister hired us to investigate Stacy's death, so I'm going over to question Gus tomorrow."

"And these are your Trojan horse?" He set the basket back on the table. "Here's a dozen gift baskets. Did you kill your wife?"

"I think I'll try more of a polite, indirect line of questioning. Honestly, I agree with the police. I think her death was an accident, but her sister is convinced otherwise."

"I can imagine it's difficult to reconcile yourself to the death of a loved one, especially when the deceased was young and the death unexpected," the judge commented. "This is probably her way of getting closure, of making sure any ghosts are laid to rest so she can mourn."

I thought of the ghost in the passenger seat of my car. "I'll do some interviews and dig through all the medical paperwork—although I'll probably have to get someone to interpret the hospital papers for me. In a few days, I'll lay it all out for Stacy's sister, and hopefully then she'll be able to accept there was no foul play in Stacy's death."

And hopefully Stacy's ghost would accept that as well.

The doorbell rang, and I heard Henry shout that he was "getting it."

"Should I move all this off the table?" I asked. We normally ate and worked in here, but I realized it would be hard to do either with the table full of baskets.

"Let's eat in the kitchen," Judge Beck suggested. "Henry can help you take them out to your car after dinner."

I quickly eyed which baskets could go back and which ones needed to stay inside the warm house, separating them accordingly. Taco returned with the arrival of our dinner. Madison filled his bowl with kibble as Henry dug some paper plates out of the cabinet and set everything up on the kitchen island. We ate, talked about homework and ideas for Thanksgiving dinner, and when we were done, Judge Beck and I sat among half a dozen baskets in the dining room, catching up on work as the kids headed downstairs with Taco to watch T.V.

By midnight, I could barely keep my eyes open. Satisfied that I'd made a serious dent in the skip trace work, I headed upstairs for bed, thinking of the appointments I had tomorrow and humming "She Took a Lot of Pills and Died."

CHAPTER 8

The Mellomaker home was in a gated golf course community on the outskirts of Milford. Even in November, the grass on and off the course was a vibrant green, the fountains on the water hazards spouting away in defiance of the cold snap. Gus must have phoned my appointment down to the gatehouse because the man bundled up in a plaid coat and heavy black gloves checked my name and waved me on through. The streets were well marked with ornate wooden signs, and with a few turns I pulled into a circular drive in front of a beautiful Mount Vernon-style home complete with curved breezeways connecting the main home to a three-car garage on the right and what I assumed was a guest house on the left.

I parked and got out of my car, suddenly realizing that I couldn't manage to carry a dozen baskets up to the front door myself. So much for the Trojan horse idea. Would I need to make a dozen trips? Were there housekeeping staff here who could assist me with all this? It seemed gauche to ask Stacy's newly widowed husband to help me cart these things inside.

I ended up just grabbing one of them—the Bear Bouquet basket—and carrying it with me, figuring I would deal with the rest later.

A man answered the door. He was bald, but in a way that made me think it was due to hair loss and not a trendy fashion style. He looked to be a bit younger than me, with casual dark slacks and a light gray crew neck sweater.

"Oh." He looked from the basket in my hand to my car that had several other baskets clearly visible through the windows. "Is that for us? I can sign for it if you want to just put it on the table over there."

He must have thought I was making a delivery. What sort of person would send a basket of stuffed bears to a bereaved family, though? Was that a thing? I always thought flowers were the appropriate offering, and those were supposed to go to the funeral home. Maybe if I were carrying a casserole…. But the Mellomakers were rich, and maybe rich people did things differently. Maybe rich people did send bear baskets and edible arrangements when someone died.

"I actually have an appointment with Gus Mellomaker," I told the man, speaking over the top of the basket. "I thought I'd bring these by since I was already coming over. These are some of the things Stacy won at bingo that night."

"Some?" The man looked from me to my car. "How many did she win? Good grief."

"Twelve." I sat the Bear Bouquet basket on the foyer table. "If you can give me a hand, I'll bring in the others."

He shook his head, looking momentarily panicked. "We don't want those things. Can you give them to someone else? Or throw them out? Honestly, we really don't need them. I've got no idea what Stacy thought she was going to do with all that stuff. What was she thinking?"

I shrugged, remembering the gleam in Stacy's eyes every time she'd shouted "bingo." I knew exactly what she was thinking. There was a high in winning, and from what I'd been told, Stacy was just the sort of individual who'd loved to win even if she really didn't drink tea or watch rom-com movies or eat cookies full of gluten.

"I'm Rick Mellomaker, Gus' son." The man put out his hand and I shook it.

"I'm Kay Carrera." I hesitated, wondering if he would have been involved in Stacy's death. With her gone, I assumed Gus' entire estate would be split between this man and Sheyanne. It was possibly a motive if Stacy's death was truly a murder.

"My father's in his study," Rick told me as he led the way. "I flew down yesterday as soon as I got the news. Honestly, I'm not that surprised. Stacy seemed healthy as a horse, but she was at one doctor or another every week getting screened for this or tested for that. I can't tell you the number of times she thought she had cancer or a rare blood disease. And the woman was on enough pills to kill an elephant. Prescriptions. Herbal supplements. Weird snake oil crap she'd gotten off the internet. No wonder she was sick. I don't think she knew what was in half that stuff, and her doctors sure as heck didn't know everything she was taking."

"So, she was your stepmother?" I asked.

He stopped mid-hallway. "Yes. And no, we didn't get along. It wasn't as if I hated her though. Dad was really lonely after Mom died, and I didn't expect him to spend the rest of his life alone. I just think he chose poorly." He shrugged. "But I'm not the one who married her. I wouldn't have been able to put up with Stacy as a wife, but that was Dad's business, not mine."

He turned and walked on before I could figure out how to reply to that. Pausing at a set of French doors, he gave them a quick rap with his knuckles, then opened them.

"Dad? Kay Carrera is here to see you."

Rick ushered me in and closed the door behind me. A trim, tanned man with thick silver hair sat, a gold framed picture in his hands. He smiled at me as he stood, waving for me to join him on the sofa. He waited to sit until I did, then put the picture down on a glass-topped coffee table. I glanced at it, realizing that the woman standing next to a much younger version of Gus was not Stacy.

"My wife, Tilly," he said with a wave at the picture. "She's probably rolling in her grave over all this. Actually, she probably hasn't stopped rolling from the moment I met Stacy."

It was the perfect opening, so I took it. "Tilly wouldn't have approved of your choice in a second wife?"

"No, she most definitely would not have approved. I can hear her now. 'Gus, I told you to not stay single after I was gone, but I expected you to have some sense about who you picked to marry next.'"

I couldn't help but chuckle at his imitation of his first wife's voice. Reaching over, I picked up the picture. "My husband passed earlier this year, so I can imagine how difficult this is for you. My condolences—on both your losses."

"I'm so sorry to hear of your loss. As for me, Tilly I still grieve. Stacy? That's more regret than grief." He turned to face me. "I know Brenda hired you to look into her sister's death. She pestered the heck out of me at the hospital until I finally phoned the Chief of Police and called in a favor. She won't give up. And she probably thinks I'm the one that did it. Lord knows I had motive."

I blinked in surprise at his bluntness. "You? What sort of motive? Not money, certainly?"

"No, not money. I was the one with all the money. I guess jealousy?" His laugh was tinged with bitterness. "Although by the time Stacy started fooling around, I was far from jealous. Relief would be more my emotion—relief that she wasn't home complaining about something or another. If she'd have run off with one of the men she was screwing around with, I would have thrown a party. Actually, despite the prenup, I probably would have paid her at this point just to get her out of my life."

I winced at Gus Mellomaker's tone. It wasn't angry or harsh; it was tired. Living with Stacy had exhausted him, and he'd clearly been happy about any moment he didn't spend in her presence.

"Why did you marry her?" Clearly there must have been something that attracted him to Stacy and kept him attracted at least for a few years of their marriage.

Gus shrugged. "I guess I wanted something new and different, something that was the opposite of the domestic bliss of my first marriage. Or maybe it was karma coming around to bite me for all those business deals where I profited off someone else's troubles. Stacy was beautiful, self-assured, confident. I felt twenty years younger with her on my arm. It was an illusion I bought hook, line, and sinker—one of me being the kind of man who a woman almost young enough to be my granddaughter could fall in love with."

"So, she really was a trophy wife," I commented, knowing full well how rude it was to say that to him.

"In a way, yes. But it wasn't just her looks and youth. When I met Stacy seven years ago, it was like looking in a mirror personality-wise. Tilly was gentle and warm, a girl I'd known and dated since we were in high school. Stacy was assertive and bold. Poised. She knew what she wanted and went after it. She didn't care who got hurt along the way as long as she achieved her goals. There was that heady rush a man gets when a young beautiful woman is on his arm. It's like we're young again—desirable and virile and exempt from the ravages of time. But it wasn't just the external trappings that drew me to Stacy, it was her personality. She was so much like me when I was first starting out. It was energizing being with her, at least at first. She made me feel as if together we could rule the world."

"At first," I commented, picking up on that part of his speech.

He chuckled. "She loved my money and the status it brought to be married to me. And in a way, I think she cared about me. Certainly, she respected me. I think if I'd been forty years younger, we would have truly had a love match, but Stacy could never get past the fact that I was an old man and she was a young desirable woman. She had affairs. And in the last few weeks, I caught her forging my name on several documents in an attempt to siphon funds off into what she thought were secret accounts." He shook his head, smiling indulgently as if recounting a tale of a naughty child.

"She forged your name? What did you do when you found out?"

"Made her close the accounts and put the money back. Put safeguards in place so that she couldn't pull that sort of stunt again." He shrugged. "I don't really blame her, you know. I'm sure Stacy was frustrated that I hadn't died a few years after our marriage like she'd hoped and left her a wealthy widow who could screw every muscular young man she desired."

"Would she have been a wealthy widow if you'd died first?" I asked.

"I have trust funds set up for my children, and Stacy would have received a comfortable sum of money upon my death."

"Which now goes to whom?" I thought of Rick in the foyer and wondered if he'd wanted more than the trust fund.

"Charity. And the contents of my will have been no secret. Rick and Stacy both knew who was inheriting what."

So much for the Rick idea. And it hardly seemed like Gus

was a viable suspect, either. "It doesn't sound like you were particularly jealous over Stacy's affairs," I commented.

He shrugged. "I wasn't, and that's a difficult thing for a lot of people to understand. Even before Sheyanne was born, our relationship had become more of a business arrangement than a marriage. But I'd made a choice. I'd married Stacy, and I'd intended to honor that commitment, no matter how many affairs she had."

I squirmed, not sure how to ask this next question. "And your daughter…?"

He shot me a wry smile. "I'm well aware that Sheyanne most likely isn't my child. I don't care what her DNA is, she's mine and I will take care of her, provide for her, and give her the same love and financial benefits that I gave Rick."

"What if Stacy had planned to take Sheyanne and leave you?"

His expression held a savage note, reminding me of the ruthless business man he must have been in his youth. "As I said, we had a prenup. Stacy would have gotten nothing in a divorce, and I would have moved heaven and earth to keep custody of Sheyanne. I'm an old man, Mrs. Carrera. I want to spend as much time as I can with my daughter before I die. And I want to make sure she's provided for, not simply used as a means to grab child support for her mother's expensive tastes."

"It really wouldn't have bothered you if Stacy had left?" I pressed, completely bewildered by this strange marriage. "If she'd run off with a younger man?"

"Absolutely not. I would have been relieved. I made a commitment which I intended to fulfill, and if I had died first, there were provisions in my will for her. I take my responsibilities seriously, and Stacy was my responsibility as long as she was married to me. But she was not an easy woman to live with. My life would have been much better had she left."

"Or died?"

"Yes, but I didn't kill her." He picked the picture up from the table. "I still see my first wife, you know. Tilly. Sometimes late at night there's a shadow out of the corner of my eye and I just know it's her. I may have bent and broken a lot of rules in business, but I never turned my back on a responsibility. Never. Tilly would have been so disappointed in me if I had. She may not have approved of my second marriage, but she would have been furious if I'd divorced Stacy or treated her poorly…or murdered her. I didn't kill my wife, Mrs. Carrera. No matter what Brenda says, I would never have harmed my wife."

I let that sink in for a moment, torn between respect for the seriousness with which Gus had taken his marriage vows and despair over how cold and impersonal their union had become.

"Do *you* think someone murdered her?" I finally asked.

Gus stared at the picture for a long while then shrugged. "No. I don't. I think her death was an accident."

I was thinking the same, but I had an investigation to do.

"Was there anyone she was arguing with recently? Anyone you can think of that might have wanted her dead?" I asked.

He turned to me with a faint smile. "Stacy argued with everyone. Endlessly. I don't know of anyone who would have wanted her dead, but I do believe that Stacy had fallen in love with someone in the last month or so. I don't know whether she was enough in love with this man to walk away from her lifestyle and all my riches to be with him, but I'm fairly certain that she was in love."

"What if this man left her or gave her an ultimatum or

something like that?" I asked. "Do you think that might have led her to overdose?"

I was totally reaching here, but in spite of her sister's insistence, I couldn't completely rule out suicide.

Gus shook his head. "No. Not Stacy. I can't see her committing suicide, even if this lover of hers walked away. I *can* see her inadvertently combining one of her herbal remedies and pharmaceuticals, although Stacy was usually very careful about such things. Perhaps one of her supplement suppliers mixed up the wrong dosage or added something that shouldn't have been there, but I don't think she committed suicide or that she was murdered. A lot of people disliked her—hated her even—but I'm not sure any of them would have gotten as far as to kill her."

"Did you know who this new man was?" I asked. "This person you thought she was in love with?"

The personal trainer at the gym, I wondered? The tax accountant who'd been a long-ago fling? Someone new? I had my doubts that Stacy had been a victim of foul play, but I still needed to track down and question any lead, just to be able to assure Brenda I'd performed due diligence in the course of my investigation.

"I've got no idea who my wife was sleeping around with." Gus' expression was tinged with sadness. "I turned a blind eye to such things. Normally we just stayed out of each other's way and only met to go over something that had to do with the household or Sheyanne, or if Stacy wanted more money."

"But you said you were sure she was in love with someone. Why? What happened to make you think this was any different than a previous lover?"

Gus glanced over at the picture again. "Stacy came to me this past weekend asking for more money. It was a sizable amount and she didn't have a good reason why she'd need that much. Between that and the recent mess with the forgery and secret accounts, I told her "no." Usually we'd end up negotiating for a smaller increase, but this time she asked me how much I'd give her if she left, if we divorced, and she didn't contest anything, if she just walked out of my life forever."

"Without Sheyanne?" I couldn't imagine someone leaving a marriage knowing that they'd be leaving their child behind.

"I got the impression she figured I'd be dead in a few years and she'd gain custody of Sheyanne then." Gus shrugged. "The only reason I can think that she'd make an offer like that was if there was someone she was in love with. I threw out a number, and she said she'd think about it."

If I didn't like Stacy Mellomaker before, I really disliked her now. She'd leave her child behind for a man, and the sticking point was the money. What a horrible person.

"You've got no idea who he was?" I asked.

Gus shook his head. "No. I'm sure there was a man, though, and that this time it was different. Stacy had always seemed satisfied with our arrangement. She had money and status. She got to be on committees and go to an expensive gym and drive fancy cars and throw parties. I turned a blind eye to her affairs. Why else would she leave all that behind?"

I mused on that for a moment and came to the same conclusion. There had to be someone she'd loved enough that she'd consider leaving her child and her lifestyle behind.

"It wasn't my business who Stacy was sleeping with, and I truly didn't want to know," Gus continued. "I didn't kill my wife, Mrs. Carrera. Being married to her was often an annoyance, but not enough of an annoyance that I'd resort to murder. Maybe this man broke up with her and she did over-dose on purpose, although I can't see her doing that in the middle of a bingo game in a public bathroom. I honestly agree with the doctors that her death was due to an accidental overdose."

Giving the framed picture one more glance, I sighed. Tilly and Gus, in happier and younger days. It reminded me of the many pictures I had of Eli and me.

"I appreciate your candor. And I truly appreciate you taking the time to speak with me when I know you're in the middle of making arrangements for your wife's funeral."

"Before you go…." He slid a folder off the coffee table and handed it to me. "These are the preliminary autopsy notes as well as the details from the investigation the detective had started on."

My mouth fell open. "You've got the police reports?"

He smiled. "It helps to know the Chief of Police. We've been friends for a very long time. I went to school with his father, was at his wedding. I'm a godparent to one of his children. Of course he gave me the reports. If you need anything else, please let me know. I truly believe this is a fool's errand, but it's Brenda's money, not mine. And if it lets her sleep at night to know she left no stone unturned in her sister's death, then I'm happy to help any way I can."

I hesitated before stuffing the folder into my bag then turned to him again. "What about *their* relationship? Brenda and Stacy? They seem so…different."

He laughed. "Not different, just two sides of the same coin. Brenda is as much of an ornery bulldog as Stacy; she's just subtler about it. They butted heads constantly. Screaming. Yelling. Threats. I've got no doubt that they loved each other, but it was the sort of love two difficult people have when they've got no one else who truly understands them."

I stood up. "Thank you for your time, Mr. Mellomaker."

He stood as well and shook my hand. "Gus. Please call me Gus."

I smiled. "Well, thank you, Gus. Oh, I almost forgot! I've

got all these baskets in the car that Stacy won at bingo. Your son said you wouldn't want them, but I thought I'd check just in case."

He waved a hand. "Take them. Keep them or give them away, or throw them in the trash. I've got enough here without twenty pounds of cookies and teas and board games."

It seemed that I was stuck with the baskets after all. A small part of me was thrilled to have them. I would have been more thrilled if I'd actually won them, but it was a tiny bit like having someone else's lottery winnings in the car and being told to keep them. I should give them out to the neighbors, J.T., Miles, and Violet.

I thanked Gus Mellomaker once more and headed out. In the hallway was a little blonde girl in a pair of mermaid-green tights and a lacy white shirt staring at the Bear Bouquet basket.

"Are you Sheyanne?" I asked softly.

She turned, sticking a finger in her mouth and eyeing me uncertainly as she nodded.

"It's nice to meet you." I walked forward and held out my hand. "My name is Kay. I know your mommy."

She shook my hand with a practiced motion. "My mommy is dead."

My heart twisted at the words. Four years old. Did she even truly understand what that meant? At that age, I doubted she realized that she'd not see her mother again.

"I know, and I'm very sorry about that."

"S'okay." She hopped from one foot to the other, sticking her finger back in her mouth and talking around it. "She'll be back at night for my bedtime song. Are these bears yours?"

I blinked back tears, hoping that the ghost in the passenger seat of my car really did come to see her daughter, and that Sheyanne grew up having wonderful memories of her mother.

"These are bears your mommy won in a game a few nights ago." I walked over and pulled the cellophane off the basket. "Do you want to see them?"

She nodded vigorously, so I knelt and brought the basket to her eye level. The finger went back in her mouth and she stared at the bears with an intense longing.

"You can take them out," I told her. "I'm sure your mommy meant to bring them home for you. They're yours now."

She glanced at me briefly before returning her gaze to the bears. "Can I pick one?"

"They're *all* yours." I balanced the basket on my knee and took out one with a pointy nose and dark embroidered eyes. "I like this one best. He looks like he's going to work all dressed in red plaid. Is he a business bear, do you think? Or maybe a lumberjack bear?"

Sheyanne took the bear from my hands and examined it. "His name is Tree," she announced.

"Well, then, he must be a lumberjack bear with a name like Tree. How about this one?" I pulled out a tiny bear with creamy yellow fur and a crown of crocheted roses.

"That's Sunshine." She reached out a hand for the bear and brought it to her face, kissing it on the nose.

"Sunshine is a beautiful name. How about this one?"

"Mud."

"Because he's got brown fur, or because he's wearing boots and a rainhat?" I asked.

"I like his boots." She took that one as well and squatted down, placing the bears carefully back into the basket with the others.

"Why don't you take the bears to your room and play with them," I told her.

She stood up, holding the basket by the handle. It was nearly as big as she was.

"Thank you," she said in a sing-song voice. "I love my bears. Thank you."

I watched her head up the stairs, taking them one at a time so as to not spill her basket of bears. Once she'd cleared the landing and I heard her footsteps retreat, I let myself out the door.

Once in my car, I headed to my next appointment with a ghost in my passenger seat, and "In My Daughter's Eyes" by Martina McBride playing on the radio.

CHAPTER 9

*D*ennis Moore was a good-looking man with light brown hair trimmed close on the sides and back, the top gelled into a swoosh that looked like it was one smoldering look from toppling into a sexy curl on his forehead. Not that the tax attorney was sending any smoldering looks my way, but from the careful cut of his clothing, the meticulous nature of his grooming, and the faint waft of expensive cologne, I got the impression that Dennis fancied himself to be a lady's man.

"Now, Mrs. Carrera." He clasped his hands and placed them on his desk, giving me a smile that was probably intended to be charming but came across as oily and self-absorbed. "What can I do to help you? Are you facing an audit? Or perhaps you need assistance in negotiating payment of back taxes?"

I might have had my share of financial woes but thank goodness I didn't have any tax problems. I hesitated, uncertain whether to concoct a lie or not. I wasn't sure how lying about a tax problem would lead to my getting any answers about this man's connection with Stacy Mellomaker, so I opted for brutal honesty instead.

Pulling my card from my purse, I slid it across the desk to him. "I'm a private investigator and I'd like to ask you some questions about Stacy Mellomaker."

He picked up the card, looked at it, then stuck it in a desk drawer, never betraying any emotion beyond the smooth self-assurance he'd been projecting since the moment I'd walked in. "I barely knew the woman. I saw her here and there at various social events, and occasionally she'd come in to drop off paperwork on her husband's behalf, but that was it."

I was pretty sure Stacy wouldn't have lied to Brenda about her affair with this man, and besides that, he was completely her type from what I could tell. Attractive. Powerful. Smooth. He exuded both wealth and the sort of professional business acumen that I assumed had attracted Stacy to Gus. The only differences were that this man was not fifty years older than Stacy, and that he was probably far less wealthy than Gus. And he was married, while Gus had been a widower and available.

"Did you know Stacy before she married Gus?" I asked, trying to feel my way around the less personal questions before I got to the ones that would most likely get me thrown out of the man's office.

"No, I don't think so. I believe I first met her at a New Year's Eve party, but I don't recall if she was married to Gus at the time or not."

"And when was the last time you saw her?"

He hesitated. "What exactly are you investigating? I heard that Stacy had died the other day. It was a complete shock to me, as I'm sure it was to her friends and family. She was young and always seemed to be in the peak of health. Does this have something to do with her estate? Is there some issue with locating funds or a question regarding her will?"

"I'm not at liberty to go into the specifics, but there are some things her family would like to clarify."

A muscle twitched in Dennis' jaw. "I saw her a few weeks ago. We were on a committee together for the library expansion."

"Did she speak to you at all during or after the meeting? Can you recall anything she might have said that indicated she was stressed or having any problems with anyone?"

Dennis let out a long, slow breath, the tension in his shoulders easing a bit. "Stacy was always stressed, and she was always having problems with someone." He rolled his eyes and leaned back in his chair. "Let's see…someone parked an SUV in the compact car spaces, so she had to go a level up in the deck to park. That was a rant that went on for at least half an hour. Oh, and I believe she was also incensed about the coconut milk in her latte that morning and was convinced that the barista had substituted dairy on purpose because she was a jealous cow, or something like that. Plus, she'd had it in for that poor girl at the library for the last few weeks. Millie or something."

"Molly?" I suggested.

"Maybe." He shrugged. "I can't remember. Basically, Stacy didn't go a day in her life without thinking someone had done her wrong or believing that she'd concocted an incurable disease that her doctors were failing to diagnose her with."

"It sounds like you didn't care much for her." Actually, I was beginning to wonder why he'd had an affair with Stacy if all she did was complain. Maybe he didn't care as long as the woman he was having sex with was beautiful with a swimsuit model's figure. Some people were shallow like that, and I got the impression Dennis Moore was very shallow. I wondered what his wife was like, and how she put up with a man like this?

Dennis leaned back in his chair. "There were plenty of people who hated Stacy, but I wasn't one of them. Yes, she could be a bit of a drama queen, but she was also smart and energetic. She got things done. She wasn't afraid to face down anyone who got in the way of a project. If she was on a committee, things happened according to schedule and on budget. I admired that in her."

"I've heard you admired a lot more than that in her." I noted his shoulders tensing again. "She told her sister that the two of you had an affair."

There was a moment of chilly silence where I wasn't sure if I was about to be tossed out the door or not.

"I'm a married man," Dennis finally said. "And Stacy Mellomaker was a married woman."

"I'm not here to ruin your marriage," I told him. "Stacy's husband was aware of her affairs and isn't concerned about any of the details or identities of her lovers. I'm merely here trying to find out if someone was angry enough at Stacy to slip a little something in her drink or food that night."

Dennis Moore flushed. The red shot up from his neck clear to the roots of his stylish hair. "I've known Stacy for years, and I can assure you that I would never have done that. I thought she died of natural causes. A heart attack or something. Someone really thinks she was poisoned? That's outrageous."

"Someone does think she was poisoned," I told him. "And you've got motive. Maybe you dumped her, and she threatened to tell your wife about the affair. Maybe she was pushing you for more of a relationship than you wanted to give."

He laughed. It wasn't one of those sarcastic villain laughs, either, but a real honest-to-goodness belly laugh. "Look, I'll deny I said any of this if you repeat it, but that's not how things went down between Stacy and me. She wasn't about to leave Gus, and I'm happily married in spite of what hobbies I may pursue in my free time. Stacy and I were too much alike to want more from each other than a night here and there. It was incredibly casual between us, and we were both happy to keep it that way. There were no threats, no pushing, nothing. No pressure. No demands. No expectations. I liked her. I admired her. But that was it. And anything between us was over years ago. I can absolutely assure you of that."

"Why? If you had a good casual thing going, then why end it years ago?"

He spread his hands outward. "The fire went out. We both got bored, and there's no sense in continuing to go through the motions. Stacy moved on. I moved on. And the only time I've seen her in the last few years has been at committee meetings."

I got the impression he was telling the truth. "So, what do *you* think happened to Stacy?" I asked. "Did she ever mention having a problem with someone? That there was someone angry enough at her to murder her?"

He shook his head. "No. But people get killed over cutting someone off in traffic, and Stacy wasn't exactly someone to hold back on her thoughts and opinions. She pissed a lot of people off. I'm sure some of those people felt angry enough to want her dead. I don't know what she died of. Hell, I thought she'd dropped from a heart attack. In my opinion, I don't think anyone killed her."

One more name to cross off my list. Dennis Moore hadn't wanted Stacy dead, and I was pretty sure he had no idea who'd killed her, if someone in fact had done that.

I thanked him for his time, headed back out to my car,

and drove to Fitness Forever, this time listening to Terry Jacks' "Seasons in the Sun."

* * *

FITNESS FOREVER WAS AN INTIMIDATING gym with shining equipment, juice bars, a lounge area full of workout apparel, and accessories for sale. Ruth Millhaven gave me the tour of the spin room, the yoga room, the free-weight room, the weight machine room, the indoor tennis court, the indoor pool, and a tall cavernous area that housed a climbing wall. Some pricey clubs skewed more toward comfort and socialization with only a nod at the trendiest of exercise equipment and classes, but Fitness Forever vowed in big purple blocky letters to provide the ultimate in workout experiences, and they took their mission seriously. The clientele was toned, shapely, and attractive, but they were also sweating like crazy in their expensive tights and sports bras.

I tried my best to not pass out when Ruth discussed the prices of the different membership options. I handed over the voucher I'd lifted from one of the bingo baskets and she eyed it, her smile stiffening.

"Oh. Well, I'm convinced after one month here, you'll be signing up for one of our membership tiers."

If only I could afford it. I really was drooling over this place, but cost aside, would I really have time to make membership worthwhile? I worked all day and often into the night. With yoga in the mornings, I doubted a pre-work gym visit would be feasible, and even if I managed to cross everything off my to-do list during the day, I liked to be home to see Judge Beck and the kids. I could definitely see myself coming on the weekends, but for the monthly membership fee, weekend visits wouldn't be enough to justify the cost. But in the meantime, I'd enjoy my trial membership guilt-free. Gus had told me to give or throw away the baskets, so I no longer had any reservations about using this trial membership as much as I could.

Ruth made a note on the voucher and put it in her pocket. "You mentioned an interest in personal training? The complimentary membership doesn't include that. Did you want me to go over costs for that as an add on?"

"Yes, please." If they were à la carte, then I'd add a couple of training sessions on as a cost of the investigation.

Ruth listed the package prices along with the cost for individual sessions and I tried to keep my expression bland as if spending that much money per hour on a personal trainer were no big deal.

"I would like to sign up for two or three sessions just to try them out before considering a package," I told her. "I'd like to use whoever Stacy Mellomaker used. She always looked amazing, and said she owed it all to her trainer."

Ruth smiled. "That's Jake. He's our most popular trainer here, and he does get results."

"Are there any openings in his schedule?" I asked.

She nodded. "We can squeeze you in as long as your time is a bit flexible. Here. Come sit in the lounge and I'll see what he has available in the next few days."

Ruth walked me back to the lounge and told me to help myself to the refrigerated case of drinks as she went to check Jake's schedule. I picked out a strawberry banana smoothie and turned to see a young man enter the lounge.

He stopped when he saw me, and there was a moment where we both smiled awkwardly.

"Are you one of the personal trainers?" I asked, because he was breathtakingly gorgeous. The young man was an Adonis, perfectly proportioned in his ripped jeans and snug tank top. He had a messy mop of curly black hair, beautiful brown eyes, and dark gold-toned skin that accented his high cheekbones, angular jaw, and full lips. I caught my breath at the sight of him, thinking that if I'd been forty years younger, I would have been an incoherent puddle before such a stunning man. Youth. Beauty. And unlike Dennis Moore, there didn't seem to be the slightest bit of vain swagger about the man. He had all the innocence and fresh appeal of Michelangelo's David.

"Oh, no." He laughed. "I'm not one of the trainers. My sister works here and I'm catching a ride home with her. Is it okay if I hang in the lounge? I'm not really supposed to be here."

I hardly needed the entire lounge to myself. "Of course you can wait here. I'm not even a member yet. I'm just getting a tour and taking advantage of a thirty-day free membership I won in a bingo game."

"Well, thanks anyway. It's kind of cold to be standing outside, and my sister locked the car." He held out his hand. "I'm Hunter."

I shook his hand. "Kay Carrera. Do you go to Milford High?"

"I graduated this past spring," he said.

Of course he had or he'd be in school right now and not here waiting for his sister to give him a ride in the middle of the day.

"So, are you in college?"

He dropped his gaze with a sheepish smile. "No. I'm working at Quick Burger. It's nice there. The people are really nice, and I get paid."

I blinked. "Well, I hope you get paid. I think it might be illegal for Quick Burger to have you work there and *not* pay you."

He laughed again and shuffled his feet before looking up at me with the innocent expression of a child. "I like getting paid. I'm trying to save up enough money to go west to

Hollywood. I want to be an actor. When I was in high school, I was in plays and people said I was really good. I think I'd be a good actor."

"I'm sure you would. Are you acting now? There's a theater group in Milford that does plays."

"I know, I know." His voice got louder, and he waved his hands around excitedly. "I talked to them. I'm going to audition if I'm not in Hollywood by the time they're ready to do their next play. I've done some commercials, too. I can put that on my resume."

"Commercials? That's impressive. So, you're already an actor." I was completely charmed by his sunny enthusiasm.

He grinned. "It was a Schaffer's Bowling Alley commercial and another ad for a local law firm. It's a start."

"Well, good luck. I expect I'll be seeing you on the big screen in a few years," I told him.

Hunter was too good to be true. Sweet. Beautiful. And not an ounce of guile about him. The cynic in me feared that this nice young man would be chewed up and spat out by the brutal film business, but the optimist in me hoped otherwise.

A young woman walked into the lounge, doing the same sort of guilty halt that Hunter had done.

"Oh. I'm sorry. I…"

"You must be Hunter's sister."

Her hair was a few shades lighter, straight and to her shoulders, but she had the same dark eyes, the same skin tone, the same high cheekbones. The effect wasn't as stunning on her as it was on him, but she was very pretty.

She nodded in reply to my question, twisting her hands together nervously. "Are you ready to go?" she asked the young man, her voice warm and full of obvious affection.

Hunter walked over to her, giving me a backward glance. "It was nice meeting you, Mrs. Carrera."

"It was nice meeting you too, Hunter," I told him.

It wasn't until after they'd left that I realized I'd seen that young woman before. She'd been the one who had been sitting next to Stacy Mellomaker at the bingo game. The one who had moved to another seat right after I'd arrived.

Ruth came back in with Jake's schedule, and I was thrilled to see he had a slot open tomorrow. I filled out all the paperwork, wrote the club a check for the personal training services, making sure I got a receipt to submit to J.T. Then before I left, I asked her who the young woman had been, the one wearing a Fitness Forever t-shirt and black yoga pants, the one who had just gotten off work to give her brother a ride home.

Ruth frowned for a moment. "That's probably one of the towel girls. They do the laundry, restock supplies, clean equipment, and get drinks and towels for our patrons. Let's see…who was here this morning? Molly. Yes, Molly was scheduled today."

Molly. No doubt the same Molly who Daisy had defended from Stacy Mellomaker the other week. The Molly who also worked part time at the library. The Molly who Stacy seemed to dislike with every fiber of her being. No wonder she'd moved seats at bingo. Had Stacy sat down next to her to harass her?

And had Stacy's bullying of the girl reached a point where she felt her only recourse was to slip something in the older woman's pot pie?

I left the gym with a temporary membership card, a personal training appointment with Jake, and the hope that Molly would be working at the gym tomorrow when I came in.

CHAPTER 10

*B*ack at the office, I managed to complete three skip trace files before I couldn't wait any longer. I pushed the folder aside and spread the reports on Stacy Mellomaker across my desk, a small pile of iced gingersnap cookies from one of the bingo baskets on a napkin to my left.

Starting with the police reports, I took out a notepad and got to work. I might loathe Detective Keeler with every fiber of my being, but the guy was thorough. He'd summarized his interviews and the reports from the hospital in nice plain English. Better yet, he'd included the list of attendees and volunteers from the bingo night. That meant I wouldn't have to go to Matt and ask for them, possibly creating a rift in the friendship we had. I didn't want to think that one of the volunteers might have been responsible for Stacy's death, but there was always the possibility that someone had reason to want the woman dead and had taken advantage of his or her volunteer opportunity to act on their impulse.

Luckily Keeler had done quite a bit of the early heavy lifting on the case, noting that the doctors suspected that Stacy had overdosed on painkillers and that it had been too long before Daisy's attempted resuscitation for Stacy to recover.

The details on the hospital report painted a grim picture, and I quickly realized that Daisy had been right. She'd been unable to restart Stacy's heart through CPR. The first responders had managed to get a heartbeat, but it had been something the reports called chemical resuscitation. When they'd loaded Stacy into the ambulance and rushed her to the hospital, she'd had an unsteady, weak heartbeat and they were still using manual methods to breathe for her. At the hospital, her heart stopped two additional times; each time it was only kept going through the drugs they were pumping into her system. Finally, a few hours after she'd been brought to the hospital, her heart stopped for the final time.

Stacy had truly died in that bathroom. Everything from that point forward had been a fruitless effort to bring her back to life.

I stared down at the slew of papers, wondering what the heck I was doing spending all this time on an accidental overdose case. Even if I shaved off some of the billable hours, I'd still spent nearly half of Brenda's retainer so far, and all I had was exactly what I'd started with. No suspects. No clear evidence that Stacy had been murdered. I was supposed to give Brenda an update on Monday morning, and I had nothing definitive to give her. The interviews with Gus and Dennis hadn't done anything except allow me to cross them off my list as far as motive went. I had nothing and I felt like I was wasting my client's money.

Cause of death. Motive. Means. Opportunity. Those were the cornerstones of an investigation, and I was coming up with zeros on all of them. The biggest hindrance right now was cause of death. I could find a dozen people who wanted Stacy dead, who had access to her medicines and who were present at the VFW that night, but unless I could somehow convince the police that Stacy hadn't taken those drugs on her own, then nothing else would matter.

So I turned to the hospital reports, staring at the incomprehensible mumbo jumbo of pharmaceutical terms. What the heck were these things? Were there interactions here that my untrained eye couldn't see? And what about levels found in Stacy's bloodstream?

I wished Eli was still alive. I could have brought this home and plopped it in front of him and gotten an honest, not-cover-your-ass, opinion. We hadn't kept in touch with many of his friends at the hospital after the accident. It had been too painful for Eli to see former colleagues, to hear them talk shop and remind him of all the things he'd never be able to experience again. But maybe I could still call one or two of them and ask for a favor for old times' sake.

I slid the reports back into the folders and set them aside with my notes, returning to the skip trace work as I mused over it all. It really *was* looking like there was no foul play. Stacy had been taking sneaky little sips from a flask. She hadn't wanted anyone to see her drinking alcohol at bingo. From what Gus and her sister had said, the woman was very concerned about her status. She didn't mind being seen as an aggressive witch, but she didn't want anyone to think she was a drunk. Or a junkie. If she'd hid the booze in the flask, there was a good chance she'd hid the more powerful of her drugs as well. If she'd gotten hooked on opiates or been an alcoholic, she would have tried to keep that hidden from everyone—her husband, her sister, her lover, and her friends.

Had there been additional drugs in Stacy's purse or coat pockets? Maybe mixed in with whatever was in her flask? Was it possible for a woman with access to a lot of money to support an opiate addiction without turning to IV drug use?

And if that was the case, then Stacy's death *would* have been accidental. I'd warned Brenda that this investigation might turn up some ugly truths about her sister. Would she regret finding out that Stacy had been an addict, keeping it all hidden from everyone?

That's when I decided to make a call.

"Tom? It's Kay Carerra. I know it's been a while, but I was hoping you could do a favor for me and interpret some medical files."

"Kay!" The warm tone in Tom's voice put me right at ease and let me know that despite not seeing or speaking with him for years, my call wasn't unwelcome. "No problem at all. When do you need to meet?"

I glanced at the clock. It was almost five. It was Friday. I'd been working my rear end off all week and was going to be taking work home with me for the weekend. I deserved to go home for the weekly porch happy hour and take a break. There probably wasn't anything earth-shattering in these files. They could wait.

"Monday morning?" I asked, thinking I could meet with Tom before heading over to see Brenda to tell her that there was no case, no murder, and that her sister had died of an accidental overdose.

"Monday it is. Eight o'clock? How about you meet me at my office?" Tom asked.

I smiled, the man's voice bringing back memories of easier times before Eli's accident. "Eight it is. I'll see you then. Thanks, Tom."

"No problem, Kay. No problem at all."

CHAPTER 11

I struggled through the narrow front door, juggling the Terrific Teas basket in my arms as Taco squeezed between my legs and made a break for freedom. I wasn't worried, knowing that if our happy hour on the porch didn't lure him home, the cat would be back for dinner, yowling at my door if he wasn't promptly let in and fed.

Leaving the door open, I walked straight to the dining room and plopped the basket down on the table.

"*More* baskets?" Henry asked as he came into the room.

"The *same* baskets," I told him. "Can you and Madison give me a hand? There are ten more in my car I need to bring in."

"Sure, but Mads is off with Dad on an errand, so it's just me." He followed me to my car. "Didn't we just take them out to your car last night? I thought you were dropping them off somewhere?"

"I did. They didn't want them, so now I'm bringing them back. I'll see if I can pawn some off on whoever comes to porch happy hour and take the rest in to work or the courthouse to give away."

"Can I have one?" he asked, balancing a basket in each arm.

"Sure." What the boy would want with a basket, I had no idea. Teas? Barbeque supplies? Bath gels?

"Cool. I get dibs on the cookie basket," he announced.

I should have known. "Make sure you share with your sister. And save some for Daisy. She was eyeing that basket all night."

By the time we'd finished, my dining room table was once more covered with baskets.

I surveyed it all and wondered once more why Stacy had been at bingo that night. She'd never come to bingo before. It hadn't been the bingo, or the pot pie, or even in support of the charity. What had made her decide to leave her fancy mansion and go to the VFW to play bingo? Hadn't she said something about unfinished business? Tying up loose ends or something like that? If so, maybe the bingo game was just a meeting venue for this other business.

Maybe there was someone in attendance that night who Stacy had come to see—someone who might have had a reason to want her dead.

I reached over to my bag and pulled out the file, looking for Matt's list of attendees and the seating charts Detective Keeler had us fill out. Maybe I'd look through these while waiting for the neighbors to come over.

So much for taking a few hours off and enjoying some wine on the porch with my friends. I eyed the folder, then shoved it back in my purse, determined to at least have a little break from work tonight.

Heading to the kitchen, I asked Henry to help me haul glasses and wine bottles out to the porch, then I grabbed some chips and a batch of espresso chip scones for snacks. The wonderful thing about it being November was that I didn't have to cart a bunch of ice to the porch to keep the wine chilled. The sad thing about it being November was that I had to haul a heater out to the porch to keep my neighbors from getting chilled.

Judge Beck had made good on his promise and had purchased a tall, propane-fueled heater like the kind I'd seen in outdoor cafés. It would have been easier to keep it on the porch during the week, but the heater wasn't exactly pretty, so I had decided to store it around the corner of the house where it would be hidden by the tall wooden gate to the backyard. Dragging the heater around the house and up the stairs to the porch was a bit of a struggle, but Henry had the harder task of carrying the heavy propane tank and setting it all up.

"Done." He fired up the heater and stood back to admire his handiwork.

"That definitely earned you some cookies," I teased. "Do you know when your father and sister are due back?"

I'd gotten used to Judge Beck joining us for our Friday happy hour. Although attendance was down with winter looming, it was nice having him hang out with us, drinking Chardonnay and chatting with my friends.

"No idea." Henry shrugged. "I think it was a shopping trip, so they'll probably be late. You know how long it takes Mads to make up her mind when it comes to buying clothes."

I nodded in agreement. "Well, if they're too late, then you and I will just have dinner without them. Pork chops and roasted veggies, or that lasagna I took out of the freezer this morning?"

"How about I just eat cookies for dinner?" His eyes twinkled with mischief and I thought how much he looked like his father when he smiled.

"How about in an hour or so you preheat the stove, put the lasagna in, and keep the cookie eating to under a dozen?" I countered.

He gave me a thumbs up and headed inside. I poured myself a glass of wine and then poured a second one as I saw Kat coming up the walkway.

"You still want that Terrific Teas basket?" I asked, handing her a glass. "And maybe one of the other ones? Except for the cookie basket. Henry's already dug into that one."

Kat frowned at me and took a quick sip of her wine. "I thought you were taking them over to Stacy's husband."

"I did. He told me to toss them. I've been driving around all day with these things in my car and they're now taking up most of my dining room table. Please, please take one of these baskets off my hands," I pleaded.

She laughed. "Okay, fine. Terrific Teas and the one with the board games, please. I like to put them in the living room cabinet for inn guests if the weather's bad."

"Awesome! I'll go grab them so you won't forget when you leave." I ran in then came back out with the two baskets, plopping them onto one of the chairs. "Let me know if you come across a flask in either of those," I told her.

She shot me a puzzled look. "In with the board games? Or the teas? Not likely. Why? Do you want a flask for some reason or another?"

"I saw Stacy drinking out of one at bingo night, but it wasn't in her purse when the EMTs went through it for her medicines. I don't know where the heck it went."

"A flask? What did it look like?"

I shrugged. "A flask. Silver colored metal with some bling on it, and I think it had engraving."

"Like this?" Kat opened her bag and dug through it before pulling out a flask.

I gasped. "Yes! Just like that. Where did you find it? Was it on the floor of the VFW somewhere? In one of the baskets?"

"This one is mine. Pastor Tim got three of them as a

freebie from a local engraving company and offered them to those of us on the church building funds committee."

I took the flask from Kat and looked it over. "An engraving company gave promo flasks to a *church*? What the heck is that about? Did they think you would drink communion wine from it? Carry around holy water?"

She laughed. "I've got no idea. They're vulgar as all get-out and terribly inappropriate for a church, so of course I grabbed one."

It did look like the sort of thing that someone would get from one of those companies that produces logo items for marketing and corporate retreats. The metal seemed thin and cheap, and the rhinestones forming a fake-diamond cross on the front were tacky. The blocky engraving across the front said, "Crossroads Community Church."

"I thought you went to Saint Paul's," I mused, wondering why Stacy Mellomaker would be drinking out of such a cheap flask.

"I was at Crossroads last year for a friend's wedding, and I really liked Pastor Tim." She pointed to the flask. "If you want it, you can have it. I picked it up because Pastor Tim clearly wanted them gone, and I thought the idea of a blingy church flask was hysterical."

It was. And if I'd indulged in hard liquor with enough frequency to want a flask, I could completely see using this one.

"I wonder why Stacy was using it," I mused. "Why keep a cheap throwaway flask like this when you've got designer bags and expensive clothing and drive a big new car? And why was she at bingo? Or on a building fund committee at Crossroads Community Church? I didn't know the woman, but from what everyone tells me, she doesn't seem the type to keep this flask, or play bingo, or spend her time on a church committee."

"Well, I can answer the last one. Stacy had money, but there are some society doors in Locust Point and Milford where it takes more than money to open. The church building fund was a big project bringing in four hundred thousand dollars for the expansion as well as a new roof on the original chapel. Barbara Stein and Ellie Proust are both members of the church and on the committee. They're old Locust Point families—old money, old connections. Respectable. Serving on the committee gave Stacy access to them. I'm pretty sure she joined the church four months ago just to get into their circle."

I shook my head in amazement. "Why did she care about Barbara Stein and Ellie Proust?"

Kat sat down in a chair and took another sip of her wine. "Stacy was the kind of woman who always wanted more. She wanted to win. Everything was a competition to her and winning one game only meant she upped the stakes on the next one. She was a mover and a shaker in her early twenties. She 'won' Gus, and that launched her from career woman clawing her way up the corporate ladder to rich trophy wife with instant connections and clout. But it wasn't enough. She would get furious if she thought someone didn't respect her or looked down on her. Throwing money around and being a total cow to service workers and small businesses only went so far. The next thing was to gain the respect of Locust Point old money—to be more than a crass, argumentative trophy wife."

I held up the flask. "And this piece of junk and bingo at the VFW were somehow going to achieve that? If her goal was to run in high-society circles, why the heck was she at bingo winning a bunch of baskets and drinking booze from a cheap flask?"

"I do know that she thought the flask was just as funny and inappropriate as I did." Kat gave me a sheepish look. "I didn't like her, but Stacy had her moments. She was funny and smart. Sometimes that came out as a razor-sharp wit criticizing someone, but sometimes she'd seem downright human and I'd feel a bit sorry for her. I always got the impression that she was a woman who'd somehow lost her way, who had spent her life desperately trying to fill a bottomless hole inside herself. I think her daughter came close to filling that hole, but even she wasn't enough. I really don't think anything would have ever made Stacy happy, no matter what she managed to 'win'."

It would have been tragic had the woman not been such a horrible person.

I took a quick sip of my wine. "When she was in line with me for pot pie, she told me she was at the VFW that night to tie up some loose ends. To finalize something or put something to rest. I can't remember exactly. You seem to know her better than anyone except perhaps her sister and her husband. Does that ring any bells with you? Do you know of any business Stacy would have had with the VFW, or anyone who was there?"

Kat frowned. "Not that I can think of, but I was too busy playing bingo to pay much attention to who she might have been talking to."

"I've got a list inside of attendees and a seating chart," I told her. "Maybe between us we can figure out who was where and see if there's anyone you might think Stacy would have had unfinished business with."

Kat shot me a puzzled look. "Why would you care? I mean, outside of mild curiosity about Stacy Mellomaker's sudden desire to take up bingo, why go through all this bother? Not to be crass, but the woman died. Her reasons for playing bingo the night of her death doesn't seem all that big of a deal."

"You talking about who I think you're talking about?"

Olive asked, climbing the stairs to the porch, Suzette right behind her. "Goodness, she's dead and that woman is still stirring up trouble."

Maybe it was intuition, maybe it was the wine, but I felt like it was time to come clean with my friends.

"I have a client who hired me to see if Stacy was murdered or not," I told them. "The doctors say it was an accidental overdose, but maybe it wasn't accidental. Or maybe I'm on a huge snipe hunt."

"Is that why you're asking about the flask?" Kat asked. "Ooh, someone might have put something in her flask! Although they'd have to be really sneaky and get it from her purse, dose it, and put it back all while she was in line getting dinner. Olive and Suzette, did either of you see anyone sneaking around Stacy's purse while we were all in line?"

"I was too busy trying to win that Crazy Coffee basket to notice anything else," Suzette confessed.

Olive frowned. "There *was* a guy going around the tables and cleaning up coffee cups and stuff. I don't think he was there long enough pour something in her flask and put it back, though. Unless maybe he grabbed it, took it back to a storeroom to pour in the drugs, then brought it back later."

"It didn't take us that long to get dinner," Kat reminded her. "Maybe the murderer drugged her pot pie instead."

"I was standing right next to her in line," I told Kat. "There's no way the man serving the pot pie could have added something to Stacy's bowl without my noticing—unless he was a sleight of hand magician."

"She got her own drinks, so that couldn't have been it," Suzette said. "It *must* have been the flask."

"And by the time the first responders got there it wasn't in her purse," I told them.

"I grabbed her coat for them to take to the hospital, and I think I would have noticed if it had been in there," Kat said.

"I don't think she would have put it in her coat pocket if she wanted it handy," Olive said. "If I was gonna sip whisky at bingo, I'd keep my flask in my purse by my side."

"So that means someone took it while we were all distracted with Stacy in the bathroom," Suzette said. "The murderer snatched it from her purse so there wouldn't be any evidence of the poison. Or drugs. Or whatever."

"But who?" I asked. "It had to have been someone at the VFW, because if the drugs or whatever had been added earlier, then Stacy would have been face down on the table before dinner was served. Something strong enough to kill her isn't going to wait an hour or so to take effect."

"And you said you had an attendee list? And seating charts?" Kat shooed me toward the front door. "Go get them and we'll see what we can come up with."

"This is the most exciting happy hour we've had in weeks!" Suzette announced before heading over to the side table to pour herself and Olive a glass of wine.

I ran in and came back out to find everyone seated around a table, wine in hand.

"Here." I plopped down the folder with the attendee list and the seating chart Matt had given Detective Keeler. We drank our wine, ate chips and scones, and took turns filling in the chart as best as we could remember while Kat circled anyone on Matt's list who she thought might have had a connection with Stacy.

On our second glass of wine, we decided to review the attendee and volunteer list first.

"I'm pretty sure we can cross you off the list, Kat," I commented. "Daisy as well." We'd been sitting together, and since Daisy and Kat had both been in line for food at the same time Stacy had, there was no time left for them to dose the woman's flask.

"Same with Olive," Suzette added. "I'm her alibi."

"Not that I think she did it, but we probably need to keep Daisy on the list." Kat winced. "I know she didn't do anything, but there was a brief moment when she was in the bathroom with Stacy before she called for 911."

I shook my head. "Not long enough to do anything. If Stacy had been bludgeoned or stabbed, then maybe, but we're going with the overdose thing, and I can't imagine anything beyond maybe cyanide that would act that fast. Besides, Stacy was in the restroom for a long time, and judging from what the hospital reports say, she most likely had collapsed a good while before Daisy even found her."

"Okay, then Daisy's off the list." Suzette took a pen to our paper as we eyed the remaining names.

"Molly." Kat sighed. "She's such a nice girl. Smart. Good-natured. Hard working. And she really takes care of that brother of hers. But she did have that run-in at the gym with Stacy, and I'm thinking there was probably recent history between them that fueled Stacy's dislike of her."

"She was sitting next to Stacy when I got to the VFW," I told them. "She moved up a few rows right after I sat down, but she *was* sitting next to Stacy for a bit."

"That's weird," Kat commented. "I can't imagine that Molly would have voluntarily been within a ten-foot radius of Stacy. And Stacy couldn't stand Molly. If the two of them were sitting together for more than two seconds, I would have expected to hear a whole lot of shouting. Maybe even some flipping tables."

"But that didn't happen," I mused. "Maybe because Stacy was there to deal with whatever unfinished business she had with Molly? That could have been what the woman was talking about in the food line."

"Possibly," Kat reluctantly agreed.

"Well, let's not jump the gun, or the poisoned flask, here,"

Olive announced, running a finger down the paper. "How about this Jake? You've got him circled."

"He's an instructor at the gym, but other than that, I don't know much about him," Kat admitted.

"Except that he and Stacy were having an affair, right?" Suzette asked.

Kat wrinkled her nose. "That was the rumor, but honestly I don't know if it was true or not. I get the impression from some friends who go to Fitness Forever that he's sexy as sin and a huge flirt. Maybe Stacy flirted back and rumors got started."

"Or maybe Jake got himself a sugar momma," Olive drawled. "Rich woman. Personal trainer, or pool boy, or skiing instructor, or golf pro at the club…"

"It's a tale as old as time," Suzette laughed.

"Maybe, but that doesn't really give him motive to kill her," I commented.

"Unless she was breaking up with him, and in a fit of rage over losing her, he…puts poison in her flask." Suzette shook her head. "No, that doesn't work."

"Besides, Stacy's husband said he thought she was in love with someone. If the rumors are true and she was sleeping with Jake, then perhaps he was the one she was considering leaving her husband for," I told them. "She leaves and shacks up with Jake, he wins. She doesn't leave but continues to be his sugar momma, he wins. There's no motive for him to kill her."

"But Gus has a motive if Stacy was fooling around and he knew it," Kat pointed out. "Especially if he thought she was going to leave him."

"The fire had gone out in that relationship a long time ago," I told her. "Gus said he would have paid Stacy to leave. Trust me, there was no jealous rage there."

"Besides, Gus wasn't at the VFW," Suzette said. "Unless he

paid one of the people on this list to poison his wife, then he wouldn't have had opportunity."

"Which pretty much leaves us with Molly." Kat sighed. "I don't see her as a killer. She's too smart for that, too nice."

"Even nice people can be pushed too far," I told her.

"But it might *not* have been Molly," Olive said. "There could be a whole lot of things that went on in Stacy Mellomaker's life that none of us knew about that could have led to her death. Molly might look like our top suspect right now, but other evidence might point us in a different direction."

"Such as this." Kat fingered the flask I'd put on the table with the papers. "Where did Stacy's flask go? The person who has it is most likely our killer."

"If there even is a killer," I reminded them. "And if there is, and he or she took the murder-weapon-flask, then they probably promptly dumped it in the VFW garbage. It's most likely on its way to the landfill right now with a ton of other trash."

"Or already there," Suzette pointed out. "Trash pick-up was Wednesday, wasn't it?"

Olive shrugged. "For residents, but places like that usually have a private service."

I sighed, hoping that I wouldn't have to crawl through another dumpster looking for evidence. At least it was November, and things would probably be less fragrant then they'd been the last time I'd gone dumpster diving.

I reached down to pick up the flask. "You said there were three of these? You have one. Stacy had one. Who got the other one?"

Kat ticked the names off on her fingers. "Me, Stacy, and Francine each picked one up. Francine just went on maternity leave this past month, and she's not on the list of attendees at the bingo game, or volunteers. Besides, if she'd been there, I probably would have flagged her down and had her come sit with us. I'd have noticed if she was there."

"Francine?" I frowned, thinking that the name sounded familiar.

"Francine Glick," Kat said. "She's a yoga instructor at Fitness Forever, and her husband owns half a dozen hotel and fast-food franchises all around the county. She's nice. Super church-going, but still fun with a great sense of humor. She thought the flask was just as hilarious as I did."

The flask. I turned it over in my hand to examine it once more. What if someone knew of Stacy's drinking problem, knew her well enough to know that she had taken to carrying a flask like this around, knew her well enough to know what sort of booze she drank? What if they'd filled their own flask with a drug-laced drink, substituting the flasks when Stacy went to go get her food or was distracted during the bingo game? Of course they would have had to really have known Stacy, known what her drink of choice was, and known that she was going to have her flask at the bingo game—even known that she would be at the bingo game.

These weren't common flasks a murderer could pick up at the local five-and-dime. There were only three that we were aware of. Which meant that either Kat or this Francine was the murderer.

I downed the last of my wine, thinking that it seemed ridiculously improbable that someone with access to Kat or Francine's flasks had pulled a switch and killed Stacy. Improbable, but all of this seemed improbable.

None of this was simple, or straightforward. *Was* Stacy poisoned? How? Why? Who? Were Kat or Francine connected somehow? Or that young woman at the gym, Molly? I suddenly wished that Stacy Mellomaker *had* died of natural causes, that the autopsy report would miraculously come in over the weekend, and I could tell Brenda there had been no foul play in her sister's death. Then maybe Stacy's ghost could rest, I could go back to my skip traces and regain control over what music I listened to in my car once more.

"I can't believe you let the kids have the cookie basket," Daisy complained, her mouth full of cookies. She'd come over after her yoga classes at Fitness Forever had ended, and we'd set an extra plate at the table so she could eat lasagna with all of us. Judge Beck and Madison had gotten home just after happy hour had ended, Madison carrying a ton of shopping bags up to her room while Henry set the table and Judge Beck made some garlic bread to go with our lasagna. Once we'd cleaned up, Judge Beck and the kids went downstairs to watch a movie while I tried to pawn some of these baskets off on Daisy.

"The kids didn't eat *all* the cookies. They saved you some," I pointed out. "Here. Have the cocoa basket instead. Or the one with the kitchen gadgets."

I was down to five baskets on my table. Kat had taken two. Suzette and Olive had taken three. I was hoping Daisy would take a couple. Maybe I could bring one in to work tomorrow and give it to J.T. Or have Judge Beck take one in for his paralegal or the bailiff. Maybe Violet Smith would want a basket.

"I'll take the grill one," Daisy announced. "I'm going to try to up my barbeque game next summer. Call it my New Year's resolution."

"One more?" I pleaded, doing my best impression of Vanna White as I motioned toward the remaining baskets.

"Okay, kitchen gadgets." Daisy gathered them up and sat them on the couch in the parlor where she'd be able to grab them before she left. Then she turned to me. "It's time, Kay. Your fairy godmother is here, and we need to do a quick evaluation and take stock of your current situation so we can begin our plan of attack."

Oh, good grief.

My friend was talking about the Christmas party I was supposed to attend with Judge Beck next month. As happy as I was for Daisy's support, I wasn't all that comfortable with her assuming this fairy godmother task. Dresses were expensive, and Daisy wasn't rich by any definition of the word. I might let myself be pressured into submitting to a highlight touch up on my hair and maybe a manicure on her dime, but I wasn't going to let her shell out hundreds of dollars for a dress I'd most likely only wear once.

"Okay, but only because I want to show you that I have plenty of suitable, nice outfits to wear and that you don't need to purchase a new gown for me. Save your Cinderella routine for a niece or yourself."

She snorted and led the way up the stairs. "As if J.T. is ever going to go to a black-tie event. Can you see that?"

"I think you're underestimating Gator Pierson," I told her. "Any man who can put on a wig and a dress to fill in for a missing extra in his YouTube series isn't going to balk at wearing a tuxedo. Invite him to that gala this spring that benefits the homeless shelter and see how nice he cleans up."

"Only if you invite Judge Beck to go," Daisy shot back.

I hushed her and looked around, wondering if the judge

could have heard her. Probably not. He was either still down in the basement watching TV or in the kitchen. My house wasn't exactly sound proof, but I doubted voices carried quite that far.

"He owes me one for this Christmas party, but I'm not ready to call that one in yet," I whispered.

"Oh, trust me, I don't think you'd need to call in any favors on this one. Just hint that you want to go, and I'll bet you dollars to donuts he runs out and buys tickets. Mention that J.T. and I are going, and that it sounds fun. Trust me, he'll do the rest."

I opened my bedroom door and ushered her in. "You're totally wrong. Daisy, I love you like a sister, but you really don't understand that this is just a friendship. I'm fifteen years older than Judge Beck. I'm his landlord. We're friends, and that's it."

"You're friends because he's in the middle of a divorce and you only lost Eli this past spring. I'll bet if you hint at it, he'll buy the tickets."

"You're wrong. And I'm not *hinting* at anything. I don't want him to think I'm some grifter trying to take advantage of his kindness or leverage my position as his landlord."

"I'm serious. Let's make a bet. Be subtle. Super subtle. Heck, just stick the flyer for the gala up on the fridge. Subtle if you're afraid he'll take it the wrong way. If he buys the tickets and invites you, then you owe me a batch of espresso chip muffins every week for a month."

"And if I win?"

"I'll buy a pair of tickets and you can take Matt Poffenberger with you."

I thought for a moment. "If I win, then you bring the wine for the next five Friday on the porch happy hours. I don't want to give Matt the idea that I'm trying to take our friendship in a more romantic direction."

Daisy rolled her eyes. "Fine. But only because I'm not-so-secretly team Judge Beck. Now let's see these dresses of yours."

I opened my closet and shoved the hangers full of shirts and pants aside, reaching toward the very far corner to pull out bag after bag of carefully stored dresses that hadn't seen the light of day in over ten years. Once they were all laid across my bed, Daisy and I stood for a moment in reverential silence, then began to unzip the bags.

The first was a red sequined cocktail dress which was a classic design, but far too young for my sixty-year-old self.

"Sheesh, was this from the last century?" Daisy held it up to her body. It came to her knees and would have been slightly longer on me.

"I think I got it in the mid-nineties for some party Eli and I went to." I took the dress from Daisy's hands and turned it around so she could see the back—or rather lack of back.

"Whoa! You sexy thing, you. Why don't you wear this?"

Daisy was clearly teasing but I still winced. "At a black-tie event full of backstabbing lawyers? Uh, no. Judge Beck wants me to be a smart, mature, socially savvy companion, not an old woman trying to look like a nineties hooker."

Daisy laughed. "Give it to Madison, then. This is the sort of dress young people are wearing nowadays."

"That hemline would barely come mid-thigh on Madison. And backless? Her father would kill me." I grinned. "Maybe I'll save it for some day when I'm really angry at Judge Beck and give it to Madison then."

Daisy laughed. "Now you're talking!"

I unzipped the next bag and held up a full-length black gown.

"Oh, no. Just...no." Daisy waved a hand at the dress. "Maybe if you're going for that Downton Abbey Dowager look."

"This is a nice dress," I protested. "I'm sure it still fits. It's formal. It's black. Black is always in style."

"Not going-to-a-Victorian-funeral black." Daisy snatched the dress from my hands and tossed it to the floor in a heap. "You vetoed the red dress, now I'm vetoing this one. Let's find something sophisticated and sexy."

"Not sleazy though," I countered.

"Not two-hundred-year-old nun either," Daisy added.

I unzipped the next bag only to immediately toss it to the floor.

"What in the name of the Lord and Lady is this thing?" Daisy scooped the mess of teal taffeta with a magenta bow sash off the floor and held it up. The dress had Joan Crawford-worthy shoulder pads and a peplum.

"Late eighties bridesmaid dress," I confessed.

"Why in the world would you keep this thing?" Daisy stared at the dress with horrified fascination. "I would have burned it after the wedding."

"It was three hundred dollars—nineteen eighty-six three hundred dollars. It's ugly as sin, but I just didn't have the heart to toss or burn a three-hundred-dollar bridesmaid dress."

"Trust me, this is uglier than any sin I've ever committed," Daisy commented. "Did you seriously think you'd ever wear it again? Or that this would somehow come into fashion in the next five hundred years? Maybe you planned to be buried in it in a crazy humorous funeral ceremony."

"It was Amy Schmidt's wedding. She was an old friend from college, and…I don't know." I laughed. "I guess I figured I'd trot it out for a Halloween party or one of those eighties parties with a worst-dress competition."

Daisy put it on the hanger and shoved it back in the closet. "Then definitely save it. Someday that eighties party is going to happen, and you'll be the belle of the ball, the big winner of the worst dress competition. Please tell me these other three bags don't have any more bridesmaid dresses, or I'm going back to the red sequined number as our top choice."

"I wasn't in that many weddings," I told her as I unzipped the next bag. Out came another black dress, this one with a keyhole neckline and an asymmetrical hem. "Uh, no. I hate these lopsided hems. This was one of those bargain, last minute emergency purchases. I figured I'd get the hem straightened out someday, but never bothered."

"Set it aside and let's see the others," Daisy chimed in. "I kind of like this one, and we can get it adjusted cheap and quick at that drycleaner's in town."

I hung the dress on the bedpost and unzipped the next bag. It was another black dress—a sheath style with long slim sleeves. "This one is nice."

"That one is boring." Daisy wrinkled her nose. "What's up with you and all the black? Outside of the red street corner 'ho and the ugly bridesmaid one, they're all black."

"Black is always in fashion. It's slimming and conservative." I ran a hand down the dress, remembering how many times I'd worn it in the past. It was comfortable, like an old friend. But I worried that it wasn't dressy enough, even though it was full length. The fabric was more of a jersey blend, and somehow, I didn't think that would be the best choice for a snooty lawyer Christmas party.

"You're one mystery dress away from wearing red sequins, Kay." Daisy pointed at the remaining bag on my bed. "Do the reveal and let's see what we've got here."

"I've got no idea what this one is," I confessed as I picked up the last bagged gown. I truly couldn't remember what was in here, which didn't bode well for the contents. If this one was a bust, I was either going shopping and spending money I didn't have on a new dress, or I was wearing the boring black one and trying to zing it up with some accessories. Saying a quick prayer, I unzipped the bag and pulled out the gown.

Daisy and I collectively caught our breaths.

"How could you possibly have forgotten *that*?" Daisy asked.

I had no idea. That bag had held a dress so elegant I swear it must have come from Princess Grace's wardrobe. It was a slim, sleeveless white gown with black geometric embroidery along the bodice. The cut. The shape. The subtle, yet bold, embellishments.

"I don't remember buying this," I told Daisy.

"Well, then, this was the best drunken purchase ever," she shot back. "I swear I saw this in last month's copy of *In Style*. Which I read in my doctor's office while waiting for my appointment, because you know I'm not the sort of woman who actually buys fashion magazines."

I hid a smile at Daisy's obvious lie. "I hope it fits."

"I've seen you in yoga pants and a tank top. I've seen you in a bathing suit. It's gonna fit." Daisy grinned. "And you're going to look amazing in it. All you need is a pearl choker, or maybe a simple chain. It's amazing. I love this dress."

I did as well, and I had been completely honest when I'd told Daisy that I had no idea where I'd bought it. Or when. I wasn't a frivolous shopper. I didn't do impulse purchases. There was no way I would have purchased this gorgeous, obviously expensive, dress and not remembered it. And unless styles had come around in the last few decades, there was no way I bought this thing fifteen to twenty years ago.

"Let me try it on, just to check." I shimmied out of my pants and shirt, eyeing myself in the mirror as Daisy unzipped the dress and slid it over my head. Part of me did feel like Cinderella, as if I was doomed to disappointment. The dress wouldn't fit. I'd be stuck with the boring black jersey or trying to find something reasonably suitable at all the discount places in Milford and the surrounding towns. Things like this didn't happen to me. I wasn't quite scrubbing floors while my stepsisters went to the ball, but ten years ago my life had changed, and I'd had no time or money or inclination for balls or parties or black-tie events.

A party, on the arm of a handsome younger man. A party where I had perfect nails and highlighted hair, and a dress that Hollywood A-listers would covet. These things didn't happen to Kay Carrera. Especially not after the accident, they didn't.

The dress fell into place as if it had been custom made. Daisy smoothed the fabric down my hips, then zipped the back with an easy motion. I turned to look at the mirror in amazement.

"Beautiful."

I wasn't sure whether Daisy was talking about the dress, or me in the dress, but either way, she wasn't wrong. I'd always considered myself a mildly pretty woman, but even without my hair done and the bare minimum of makeup on, I looked amazing. The dress hugged my slim figure, the black embroidery making my bosom look larger and more perky than any sixty-year-old woman had a right to. My legs looked so long, my waist so small, my shoulders and arms tanned and toned. It was a magic dress, and I couldn't believe this had been in the back of my closet for the last fifteen or twenty years.

Or had it?

I picked up the bag, eyeing the store name printed on the inside. Bakersville's. It was a boutique store in Milford. I knew that because I'd seen the store when I'd been downtown last. It had only been in business for a year, and I was absolutely positive that I'd never shopped there.

I'd not bought this dress.

Sometime in the last year this dress had made its way into my closet. Eli had been basically house-bound for the last ten years. If he'd asked someone to buy the dress as a gift for me in the months before he'd died, then why had it been stuck in the back of my closet and not in a box with a big bow on it?

Someone bought this dress, and it hadn't been my husband. Had his ghost, a spirit that wasn't more than a shadow at the edge of my vision, managed to swipe a dress from a ritzy store? Or did I truly have a fairy godmother?

I eyed Daisy suspiciously. "Did you buy this and sneak it up here?"

My friend was skilled at a lot of things but lying wasn't one of them. Daisy blinked in surprise. "No! I was fully prepared to veto all your dresses and haul you out shopping where I'd proceed to convince you to let me pay for a dress. Are you sure you didn't buy this and just forgot about it?"

"In the last year? Because that's how long this store has been open." I showed her the logo inside the bag. "I wouldn't have spent money on a formal gown while I was grieving the death of my husband and worried about paying the mortgage. No, I didn't buy this."

We both turned to the bedroom door at the same time, the pair of us simultaneously coming to the realization that there was someone else who might have bought the dress.

I felt my face flush hot with embarrassment. "I'm taking it back."

"Then I'll just buy it for you." Daisy glanced at the label. "Or maybe not. That place is crazy expensive."

"I know. Why would he do this? He had to have known I would refuse, or he wouldn't have hidden it in the back of my closet with the other dresses." I was mortified. Did he think I lacked a suitable gown? That I'd be an embarrassment to him in some old rag? It fit perfectly. How had he known what size to get? Oh, Lord. The man had been up here in my bedroom, going through my closet to find my size. And then back up here to hide the dress. Now I was embarrassed *and* a bit angry.

"Maybe he had Madison help him," Daisy said, clearly knowing where my thoughts had gone. "Don't be insulted, Kay. Men like to do nice things for women. I'm sure he meant this as a thank you for agreeing to go with him and not a slight on your lack of formal outfits *or* your lack of funds."

I wasn't sure what was worse, the idea that Judge Beck was rooting around in my closet, or the idea that Madison was in on this whole thing. "Why didn't he just give it to me as a gift? I'm more upset about him hiding it in my closet then if he'd handed me a box and said, 'happy early birthday' or something."

Daisy shot me a knowing look. "Seriously? He hands you a box with an expensive dress in it, and you would have handed it right back to him. You would have felt it was an inappropriate gift for a tenant to give his landlady. You would have been offended that he thought you didn't have something suitable to wear. You would have shoved the box right back into his hands and demanded that he return it. Then there would have been this awkwardness between the pair of you for weeks or months."

I glanced at the closet. "I don't like the sneakiness of this."

Daisy laughed. "Oh, come on. You've got to admit it was a brilliant plan. If you hadn't have seen the store name inside the bag and known it was only opened this year, you would have completely believed this was an impulse purchase from fifteen years ago that you'd forgotten about."

She was right. I bit my lip, undecided on what to do. I *should* take this dress back, but then I'd either be stuck with a store credit or a wad of cash that I was pretty sure Judge Beck would refuse to accept. And if the store just reversed the charge on his credit card, he'd know. Then he'd know that I knew. And I'd know that he knew that I knew and there would be that awkwardness Daisy mentioned.

Or I could keep the dress and pretend that I thought I'd bought it years ago and forgotten about it. He'd be thrilled that he'd sneakily managed to get me to accept a gift. And if Madison was in on it, she'd be thrilled that the scheme had worked.

"Keep it. Wear it," Daisy urged. "Every woman deserves a fairy godmother, and if that fairy godmother is a smoking-hot judge, then all the better."

I ran a hand down the lines of the dress, looking over at myself in the mirror. I'd refused to let Judge Beck buy the replacement dishwasher—I'd refused to even allow him to loan me money for the replacement dishwasher. But this was different. My going to this party benefitted him, and if this was his way of showing his thanks, then maybe I should remove that stick from my rear end and play along.

"Okay. You win. I'll keep the dress." I smiled as Daisy gave a silent cheer. "But not a word to anyone about this! As far as you and I are concerned, I bought this years ago and forgot I had it in my closet. Agreed?"

Daisy grinned. "Agreed."

CHAPTER 13

Saturday morning, I skipped yoga and headed into Fitness Forever. The gym was packed, even at six. Most of the patrons were up in the spin class and using the weight machines, so I swam in the amazing pool. After a dozen or so very slow laps, I went to climb out and found Molly standing by the edge, holding a towel out to me.

It was heated. After I dried off, she took the towel and handed me a robe. It was heated as well.

"Thank you," I told the woman, wondering if I was supposed to tip her. I was wearing a swimsuit. It wasn't like I had a bunch of ones in a plastic baggie shoved into the neckline. Maybe I was supposed to tip her before I left? Or once a week?

"Are you the new member?" She smiled at me. "You're the lady I saw in the lounge yesterday afternoon. Mrs. Carrera, right? I looked you up on the internet and saw you're a private investigator. I also read that your husband passed away this last March. I'm so sorry to hear that. He was a surgeon, right?"

Holy cow, this young lady had done more fact-finding

work before sunrise then I'd done in the last twenty-four hours. I wondered if she'd run a credit check on me as well or done a case search?

"Please let me know if I can get anything for you today—juices or a cucumber spritzer, or a yoga mat. There are baskets with shampoo, conditioner, and bath gel in the locker room for when you're done with your workout and ready to shower. I'll have heated towels ready for you when you're done," she continued without waiting for an answer to her questions. Not that I needed to answer them. She'd clearly Googled the heck out of me in the wee hours of the morning.

I repeated my thanks and looked around. "Where should I put the bathrobe? Is there a bin in the locker room?"

"Just leave it wherever. I'll collect it and take it to laundry," she told me.

"You do this for all the members? You must be running around like crazy handing out towels, restocking shower supplies, and picking up after us all." I snuggled into the warm robe, thinking that I better not get too used to this sort of thing.

"It's not bad for a part time job. And people sometimes leave tips in the jar in the locker room."

Tip jar in the locker room. I got the subtle message loud and clear and made a mental note to put a few dollars in before I left. "I'm sure you have to deal with a lot of jerks, though. Like that Stacy Mellomaker. I heard she was a member here."

Molly looked down, but not before I caught a surprisingly steely glint in her eyes. "Most people are very nice," she prevaricated.

Diplomatic. And not meek. "I heard about the run in you had with Stacy the other week. I heard she wasn't nice to you at the library, either."

She made an exaggerated shrug. "Mrs. Mellomaker took a dislike to me. I'm not sure why. Either way, I'm sorry that she died."

Now *that* was a lie—both being sorry that Stacy was dead and the part about not knowing why the other woman disliked her so. There was more here than Stacy just being her usual abrasive self. What had gone on between these two?

"Why were you sitting next to her at bingo on Tuesday if she disliked you so much?" I asked.

Molly jerked her head up, meeting my eyes for a brief panicked moment before lowering her gaze again. "It was the only free seat. I moved as soon as another one was available."

There had been plenty of free seats at bingo that night, but it was clear Molly wasn't going to tell me the real reason. I pressed on, figuring I might up the pressure just a bit and see if I couldn't get her to reveal what was truly going on between her and Stacy Mellomaker.

"The police are thinking her death might not have been accidental," I lied. "I heard they think someone killed her by slipping drugs into her food or drink."

Molly caught her breath, tightening her grip on the towel. "Well, it wasn't me. Maybe they need to talk to that new yoga instructor. They really got into it last week. People complained because she was yelling at Mrs. Mellomaker. If anyone killed the woman, it was probably her."

I couldn't believe Molly had just thrown poor Daisy under the bus, and after my friend had intervened on her behalf. This young woman obviously had secrets, and she was nervous about being blamed for Stacy's death. I'd need to find out what really was between the two of them, and clearly Molly wasn't going to tell me. It was a good thing I had a month's free membership here to find out. People gossiped, and people especially gossiped in health clubs like this. I was sure someone here knew what had happened between Molly and Stacy. And if not, I was pretty sure Kat could point me in the direction of someone at the library who might know.

Molly hurriedly repeated her offer to get me juices or a yoga mat, then took off with my damp towel clutched tightly. I headed into the locker room to change into my workout clothes, folding the robe and leaving it on the end of one of the polished wood benches. Then I went to meet Jake for my personal training session.

Jake Gistman was completely different than Dennis Moore. I wasn't sure why I assumed that Stacy would have had a type, but I had. Dennis was meticulously groomed, ambitious, calculating—the male version of Stacy. Jake was like something on the cover of a romantic thriller novel. He had a rugged attractiveness about him—short dark brown hair, a five o'clock stubble at seven in the morning, and a body that looked like he was fully capable of lifting an entire rack full of weights. Even with his shorts and tank top, I could tell every inch of the man was sculpted muscle. He introduced himself with a grin that hinted at wild, rough sex in a remote snow-covered cabin.

"Mrs. Carrera." His voice rumbled deep in his broad chest. "Tell me about yourself and what you'd like me to do."

I suddenly realized that his statement held a whole lot of meaning. Or did it? It had been decades since a man had come on to me, and I didn't really trust my judgement. Maybe this was part of his work persona—make older women feel desirable so they put more into their workouts and scheduled more personal training sessions with him.

"I like to think I'm in reasonably good shape," I told him, "but the other day I jogged half a block and felt winded. I want to be a bit more toned as well. And women my age should probably be doing weight-bearing exercises. Osteo-porosis runs in my family, unfortunately."

His hot gaze raked down my body. "Oh, I'm sure you don't need to worry about that, but a good weight routine can do wonders for a woman. And your husband will love the effect a few months of deadlifts and squats have on your posterior."

No woman feels confident in her posterior. I was already wondering if I could manage to scare up money for a few months of training. Not that I had a husband to notice.

"I'm a widow. My husband, Eli, passed in March," I told Jake.

That smile curled up the edges of his lips again—the smile that made me think he was contemplating hauling me over his shoulder and dragging me off to a cabin in the woods.

"I'm willing to bet you won't be a widow for long. Now let's get started here and see if we can improve on perfection. I can't imagine what I could do for your body besides worship it, but I'll promise I'll provide every service I can."

Okay, the guy was laying it on a bit thick, although I felt myself blush at his words. No wonder people flocked to this gym and paid the big bucks for membership and personal training sessions if this was what they got. A buff man flirting with you as if you were the next Playboy model? A young woman who would run and get you heated towels and juices with a wave of your hand? This was paradise—a brief fantasy on a Saturday morning.

Jake reached out to take my arm. "Let's start with measurements, shall we? That way we can properly evaluate progress at the end of the month. There's a private room back here where we can go."

I held back a second, wondering nervously whether "measurements" included more than "measurements." Was this part of Jake's services, and if so, did the club know that he was providing more than the standard personal training services?

Let's call it shock, or perhaps my investigative duty, but I let Jake lead me into a small room with a scale, a basket of measuring tapes, a bunch of clipboards, and what appeared to be a very comfortable couch. A series of lockers lined the wall, one of them secured with a small blue padlock.

I got measured. And I felt like a deer in headlights for the whole process. Jake was professional but skirted the line of intimacy with every brush of his hands. Fingers lingered just a second too long. His head moved a bit too close to read the numbers on the tape. His warm breath brushed against me as he whispered the measurements before writing them on a paper attached to a clipboard.

It had been a very long time since a man had paid this sort of devoted attention to my physical self. Eli adored me. I had no doubt that he'd loved me since the moment we met. His spirit lingering each evening in our home was proof of the enduring nature of our marriage. But after the accident, our relationship had shifted in a very different direction, and this very sexy man's hands against my thighs and waist and chest and arms were spurring a whole lot of tingling feelings that I'd rather not have.

"I've got some great ideas for workouts," Jake told me, eyeing his clipboard.

The trainer led me out into the gym and guided me through a set of exercises, all the while remaining close to me, his hands occasionally giving assistance that I wasn't sure was necessary. After an hour, I was sweaty, stinky, and more flustered than I'd been in a long time.

Jake was a great trainer. I'd pushed myself beyond what I'd thought I could do, and he had known the exact machines and weight routine to target all the areas I wished to tone. I didn't have any illusions of reversing time and becoming the woman I'd been in my twenties, but a fit and strong sixty was definitely my goal. And I'd really like to be able to jog down to Suzette's or Kat's house without feeling winded.

And the rest? Well, it was incredibly flattering to have this very testosterone-fueled younger man focus all his attention on me. But that was all an illusion, a way of ensuring I forked out every dime I had for training sessions. I wasn't a fool.

Before I left, Jake gave me an intense look, taking my hand in his and telling me that he looked forward to seeing me tomorrow. I quickly calculated how many training sessions I had left before I needed to say goodbye to Jake and his assistance. I'd need to act fast, or Jake wouldn't have any incentive at all to answer my questions.

"I want to ask you something," I said in what I hoped was a warm voice. "Stacy Mellomaker told me that you were her favorite trainer, that she owed every bit of her fitness and amazing figure to you."

An odd combination of expressions flickered across Jakes face. Regret? Anger? Pride?

"Six years I worked with Mrs. Mellomaker," he told me. "Six years. And I'm glad she was happy enough with my services to recommend me to you. I look forward to seeing you tomorrow, Mrs. Carrera."

He left and I watched him go before turning to head into the locker room, two thoughts running through my mind. One, that I was pretty certain the rumors of Jake and Stacy being lovers were true. And two, that six years was a very long time to share someone's bed and not let your heart get involved.

Molly was true to her word. There was a nice basket loaded with all sorts of high-end products right outside the shower area. A few women were drying their hair. One was putting on makeup at a table that looked as if it should be in an A-list celebrity's dressing room.

"You new?" one of the women asked as I selected from among the dozens of shampoos and conditioners. "I'm Babs Tandy."

"Kay Carrera." I shook her hand and turned back to the shampoos. "Any idea which of these works best for sweaty, chlorinated hair?"

"Salt water, not chlorine." She chuckled. "Sweetie, if they used chlorine in that pool, half the bleach blondes in here would have green hair. Here, use this one. And this one."

"Thanks." I turned to her. "I signed up for some personal training sessions with Jake. Is he the best? Are there any other instructors or classes you'd recommend?"

"Jake will whip your butt into shape faster than anyone," Babs told me with a wag of her finger. "He'll also empty your wallet and have you thanking him for the privilege. That man could sweet talk the Pope himself into sin. Mmm, mmm. But besides being serious eye candy and a huge flirt, he's a good trainer. Pricey, but good. That new yoga instructor is really good too. We were all a bit worried when Francine went on leave, but her replacement is amazing. Josie who runs the spin classes is good, too."

"Thanks." I lingered a moment, holding the shampoo and conditioner bottles. "I wasn't sure about Jake. I mean, I'd heard that he and Stacy Mellomaker had something going on, but he was recommended, so I thought I'd give him a try."

"Did you know Stacy?" Babs shook her head. "Can't exactly say many people are sorry she's gone. As for her and Jake…there were a lot of rumors. I know she wanted him bad when she'd first joined the club."

"Six years ago?" I asked, thinking of Jake's comment.

"Yep. She probably spent a fortune in personal training with him. I'm pretty sure she was trying to lure him into some other sort of arrangement, but I don't know if he took the bait or not. Who knows how much of their flirting was

Jake being Jake and Stacy trying to get everything she wanted."

"How about Molly? I heard she had a run in with Stacy last week. Any idea what that was about?"

Babs rolled her eyes. "Everyone in the club heard Stacy screaming at that poor girl. Stacy's towel probably wasn't warm enough, or the girl forgot her smoothie or something. She's a good kid. Works hard. I figured Stacy would complain and they'd fire the kid. That's what happens when you've got money. You grumble about something and heads roll."

An odd statement, given that Babs probably also had money or she wouldn't be a member of this club. I thanked her and headed into the shower area, thinking over the woman's words as I lathered up in a private shower stall lined with cedar planking and featuring adjustable pulsating jets. If Stacy had complained, then Molly would have gotten fired.

Maybe. People complained and Daisy hadn't gotten fired, but a qualified yoga instructor was a bit harder to replace than a towel girl. People had been murdered for less, but in the end, Molly was still working here. She hadn't lost her job, and I couldn't imagine her going through an elaborate murder plot just because someone yelled at her.

I finished my shower and dried off with a warm towel, slipping into another warm robe before exiting the shower area. There, restocking hair products by the blow driers, was Molly. She studiously ignored me as I dressed, fiddling with the bottles on the table and recoiling the cords on the blow driers.

"Can I talk with you?" she whispered as I came over to dry my hair. "Outside. In the parking lot?"

"When?" I asked, my heart racing as I wondered what sort of secrets this young woman might reveal.

"Twenty minutes?" She glanced over at the makeup table. "Or thirty?"

I rarely wore more than a quick dash of mascara, and my hair didn't require anything besides a quick blow dry. I wouldn't need thirty, or even twenty, minutes. "How about ten?"

She nodded, her gaze lowered. "Okay. I'll be out by the blue Ford pickup at the end of the parking lot."

I dried my hair as she left me alone in the locker room. It didn't even take ten minutes for me to finish, grab my gym bag, and speed-walk for the door. Molly was standing next to a battered truck with a *No Farms, No Food* bumper sticker on the back. The tailgate was secured with a bungee cord and bits of hay were wedged in the sides.

"Did Mrs. Mellomaker really get murdered?" She twisted her hands together. "Poisoned? Are you investigating it? Am I a suspect? Are they going to arrest me here at work? I'll lose my job. They'll fire me, and I don't make enough just working at the library."

The woman looked like she was about to cry. Her panic went a long way toward convincing me of her innocence, and I began to feel guilty for lying and scaring the girl.

"The police aren't coming to arrest you, but you've got to admit that you seem like a suspect, Molly. Clearly there was bad blood between you and Stacy, and you were next to her at the bingo game. You could have slipped something in her drink when she wasn't looking or when she got up to get food."

"I didn't! It wasn't me!" Molly's voice rose, and she looked around in panic, dropping the volume back to a near whisper. "I just told her if she didn't leave Hunter alone, I was going to post the pictures all over social media."

My eyebrows shot up. "Hunter? Your brother Hunter? What was she doing to your brother? And what pictures?"

"That woman was obsessed with my brother," Molly snapped. "He's eighteen. I know it's not illegal or anything, but he's eighteen and she's probably almost forty."

I winced because she'd said forty as if it were an unfathomably ancient age.

"Hunter's a little…he's always been naïve when it comes to people and that woman was taking advantage of him. She was promising she'd buy him an apartment and a car."

"Could he not tell her 'no'?" I asked. "Was she threatening him? Did she force him?"

Molly snorted. "Right. As if any guy is going to say 'no' to a hot older woman wanting to sleep with him and buy him things. I saw what was going on, and it's wrong. She's married. She's a shallow nasty person. And she's old."

"So you threatened her? Said if she didn't leave your brother alone you were going to post these pictures? Pictures of her and your brother having sex, I guess?"

"What? Ew, no, that's gross. Why would I have pictures of my brother having sex with someone? And I wouldn't want naked pictures of my brother on the internet even if I did. No, I told her I had pictures of her drunk and passed out and of her pouring booze from a miniature into a smoothie. I told her I'd make sure all the snooty women on her committees had a copy, as well as everyone in the gym."

"You had pictures of Stacy Mellomaker drunk?"

"No, but she didn't know that. She hated me because I told her to stay away from Hunter, but when I threatened to post pictures of her drunk, she blew up. That's when we had the big fight in the fitness center last week, the one where she was threatening to get me fired from both my jobs, saying no one would believe a cheap piece of trash like me over her, that she'd claim they were doctored or fake and no one would believe me. She said she'd sue me, make sure no one hired me ever, and ruin my name. That's when the new yoga instructor got between us and told Stacy to leave me alone."

"But Stacy didn't get you fired," I mused.

"No, she didn't." Molly lifted her chin, that defiant glint back in her eyes. "Guess she really thought I had pictures and decided her reputation was more important than getting revenge on me."

"And did she leave your brother alone after that?" I asked.

Molly shook her head. "A few days later, I find out it's even worse. Now she's not just trying to make my brother into her boy-toy, she's hinting she wants to run away with him."

"What does Hunter say about all this?" I thought of how beautiful he was, how he'd seemed almost childlike in his innocence.

"He thought that she was going to take him to Hollywood with her, sponsor him, and introduce him to movie stars. He thought she was going to get him a career in movies. But I knew better. I overheard her at the gym saying that she was going to this bingo night and I decided I was going to straighten this out once and for all."

"If threatening Stacy at the gym had her screaming in your face, then why was she so calm at bingo that night? It didn't seem like the two of you were having any sort of argument that I could see."

Molly let out an exasperated breath. "No, we weren't. I threatened her with the pictures again, and she told me she didn't care. Said she loved Hunter, and that they were going to run away to California together. She said her husband was going to give her a bunch of money if she left and divorced amicably, and that she and Hunter were going to take Hollywood by storm." Molly's lips curved down and trembled. "I think she might have really loved him. Hunter isn't careful when it comes to other people. My biggest fear is that he'll save up enough money to go out to California, and he'll get robbed and preyed upon. I don't want my brother hurt, but he's a grown man and can do what he wants. At least that woman would have made sure no one took advantage of Hunter. She probably would have made him a star just out of sheer determination and orneriness. And if she loved him… well, I guess that's the best I could hope for. So, I told her that if she hurt my brother or left him, I'd hunt her down and kill her. Then I moved up a few rows and played bingo for the rest of the night."

I stared at the young woman, absolutely astonished at the story. Stacy Mellomaker and Hunter. Her husband and her sister had been convinced she was in love with someone, and it seems it was true. Stacy was going to take the money Gus offered her, leave her daughter behind, and run off to California with a beautiful eighteen-year-old man.

And less than two hours after announcing her intentions to Molly, she was dead on the bathroom floor of the VFW. Unfortunately, it seemed no one had more of a reason to want her dead than this young woman before me.

"I had motive," Molly said, her voice wavering. "And I'd threatened her. People knew she hated me, heard the argument in the gym. I was at bingo that night. I'd been sitting next to her. They're going to arrest me. I'm going to go to jail. Then who will take care of Hunter? Our dad died when we were ten, and we live with Mom, but what happens when she dies? Hunter is so good looking, and he trusts people who he really shouldn't trust. Who will look out for him and keep him safe when I'm in jail?"

"No one's going to arrest you. At least not yet." I thought for a second. "We just have to figure out who else had a motive to murder Stacy. *If* she was murdered, that is."

Molly stared at me in surprise. "But you said she'd been poisoned, that the police were investigating."

"*I'm* investigating. The doctors at the hospital think she died of an accidental overdose."

Molly glared at me. "You lied. You told me she was murdered, and the police were investigating. You had me afraid that I was going to be arrested. That woman probably did overdose. She was always thinking she was sick. Between that and her drinking, it's no wonder she overdosed."

"Her family thinks otherwise. They think someone poisoned her."

Molly rolled her eyes. "Well, the family is in denial. Won't be the first time that's happened."

"And if they're right and Stacy was poisoned?" I let that sink in for a moment. "What if autopsy reveals that someone slipped her something? You'll be the first one the police come for."

She paled, then straightened and took a step backward. "Well, that's not going to happen because she didn't get murdered. She took too many pills and died, and it was an accident. And I'm...I'm not talking to you anymore, so go away."

She ran into the gym, and I stood in the parking lot staring after her, hoping again that the Medical Examiner ruled that Stacy's death had been an accident. Otherwise this girl was going to be in a lot of trouble. I knew in my heart Molly hadn't killed the woman, but I doubted Detective Keeler would feel the same.

CHAPTER 14

I spread out my work on the dining room table and spent the afternoon trying to get ahead on the skip traces. Judge Beck and the kids were off at a basketball game and everything was quiet except for Taco purring in the chair next to me, so I was startled when the doorbell rang.

It took me a few seconds to get over to the door. I wrestled it open and was surprised to see Detective Keeler standing on my porch.

"You should get one of those peephole things," he told me. "I could have been a burglar, or a rapist and you just threw open the door like you're living in Mayberry or something."

Locust Point *was* pretty much like Mayberry. At least I'd always thought it was. This past year, working for J.T., seeing ghosts, and solving murders had made me realize there was a lot going on in my little town and the county than I'd ever imagined. Perhaps the detective was right, and I needed to take my safety a bit more seriously.

The thought made me sad. People should be able to just

open their doors on a Saturday afternoon without fear of who might be on the other side.

"So, you dug up my address and drove here from Milford just to chastise me on my home security?" I asked.

He ignored my jibe and gestured to the door. "Can I come in? I need to talk to you about something."

His serious tone sobered me right up. I ushered the detective in, pointed him to the couch in the parlor, and offered him coffee or perhaps some cinnamon coffee cake.

He hesitated at the cinnamon coffee cake, then shook his head and got right to the point. "I know you've been investigating Stacy Mellomaker's death, and I'd like your notes as well as any insights or leads you might have on the case."

My heart skipped a beat and I sat down in a chair opposite him. "Did the M.E. rule it a murder?" There was only one reason Detective Keeler would take time out of his Saturday, drive out to my home, and ask for my notes.

"Let's just say that my investigation is off the back burner and now at the top of my stack. In the interests of saving time as well as bringing the person responsible to justice as quickly as possible, I'd like to have your notes on the investigation."

"My client hired me to investigate, and I'm not sure if I can share this information with you or not. I should probably check with her first."

I was stalling. Brenda would absolutely want me to share with the police if her sister was in fact murdered. The truth was, I didn't feel I had anything concrete to give Detective Keeler, just a lot of guesswork about a missing flask and some conjecture about who at bingo that night might have had a reason to want Stacy dead. It wasn't like I had a smoking gun in hand or a poison-filled flask, as the case might be.

Besides, I kept thinking of Molly in the parking lot,

scared and near tears. She was the top suspect if I looked at all this objectively, but I felt in my heart it wasn't her.

Maybe I was wrong. Maybe she'd spiked Stacy's drink, hoping to just give her a bad case of the runs and whatever she'd given the woman had interacted with her medicines. I thought of Peony serving a year for manslaughter and felt sick. I didn't want that to happen again. Molly was eighteen. Her sentence would most likely be a whole lot more than a year in a detention facility.

"How exactly did Stacy Mellomaker die?" I asked the detective. "If you can tell me what the M.E. said, let me know what sort of poison or drug it was, then I might be able to help you. Otherwise all I've got is a whole lot of preliminary notes and I'm not turning those over to you without a warrant or my client's permission."

Detective Keeler scowled. "It was a drug overdose, but not one of the drugs found in her purse or one that had been prescribed to her."

"Not a street drug, then?" I asked. "Clearly it was something unusual or you would have continued to think Stacy was a user and this was an accidental overdose."

"Possibly something available off the street for the right price and with the right connections. It's not something that was prescribed to her or that she would have had easy access to," he said.

I'd been thinking of her food and her drink, of her flask, but maybe someone had switched her pills. Had I seen her take any of those pills? No, I hadn't. Stacy would have seen someone dosing her drink, and I was right there when the volunteer dished the pot pie into the bowl for her. No, it had to have been added either to a drink left on her table or her flask.

Olive had said a volunteer came by while we were in line

and cleaned up the drink cups. Plus, Stacy had brought a fresh drink back with her food.

"Remember I said Stacy had a flask in her purse? She'd been drinking from it earlier on, and I remember her drinking from it when we'd gotten back from getting our food. I'm pretty sure that's the only place someone could have added the drugs."

"A flask?"

I nodded. "And it wasn't in her purse when the first responders were looking for her medicines. Or in her coat. Or in any of the baskets she'd won that were at her table. It was gone. I saw her take a few swigs before she headed to the bathroom, so it should have been there. Someone removed it in all the chaos of finding Stacy on the bathroom floor. Someone went over to her purse and took the flask."

Keeler sighed. "I'm going to have to talk to every person who was at the bingo hall. Someone had to have seen someone spiking Stacy Mellomaker's flask."

"Or going through her purse," I mused. "That's what I don't understand. Women have purse-radar. I'm pretty sure we would have noticed someone going through another person's purse."

"If the flask was on top where it was handy, then it could have been quick," the detective pointed out. "Especially with all those baskets on her table. The killer would have acted as if he or she were delivering a basket or cleaning up used cups and plates, dropped something on the floor, and grabbed the flask while picking it up."

"I thought of that, but then the person would have to go hide out in the bathroom and dose the booze, then return and slip it back into the purse. There wasn't much of a window of time for that while we got food, and I think people would have noticed someone going back again to a table they'd just cleaned off."

I thought again about what Olive and Suzette had told me during happy hour. "My friends had a clear view of Stacy's table while Kat, Daisy, and I were up getting food. They did say a man came by to clean up cups."

"But did he come back? Your friends would have noticed if he'd lingered long enough to slip something in the flask, wouldn't they?"

I pursed my lips in thought. "What if he swapped flasks? The flask was one given out by a church. They were pretty distinct and engraved with the church name but there were three of them and they were identical."

"A church was giving away *flasks*?" Keeler interjected.

I shushed him and continued. "Three flasks. One Stacy Mellomaker took. My friend Kat took another. It's been in her purse but empty since she got it. And she was in line for food with us, so it wasn't her."

"Maybe someone stole it from her," the detective said.

I shook my head. "She pulled it out of her purse Friday evening. Here. I've got it over here." I stood up and went to get the flask, opening the top and taking a sniff. "Nothing. It's never been used from the smell of it."

I handed the flask over to Keeler who did the same, then put it in his pocket. "You're sure this was exactly the same as the flask Stacy Mellomaker was drinking from that night?"

"Positive. They're pretty distinctive."

"Who has the third?" he asked.

"The yoga instructor from Fitness Forever. Francine. She's been out on maternity leave."

Detective Keeler scowled. "Whoever did this knew Mrs. Mellomaker would be at the VFW that night, knew that she carried a flask and exactly what she put in it, *and* they had access to either this Francine's flask or knew enough about Mrs. Mellomaker's to have a duplicate made. *And* they had motive to murder her."

I blinked, realizing I hadn't thought about someone making a copy of the flask. It was from one of those companies who did corporate logo giveaway products, so it wouldn't have been hard to order a new one. "If he or she had a duplicate made, then they knew a few weeks in advance that they were going to kill Stacy," I pointed out.

Keeler nodded. "So, I'm going to assume someone had access to this Francine's flask. I'll need to get her last name and call on her to see if she still has it or knows when and where it went missing."

I made a quick note to get Francine's last name and number from Kat, squirming as Keeler pulled out his list of attendees and volunteers from that night.

"The links here are the bingo game, the fitness center, and this church where Mrs. Mellomaker got the flask."

He drew a few circles on the paper, making it look like a Venn diagram. I leaned over and saw he'd underlined three names—Daisy, Molly, and Jake.

It wasn't Daisy. It wasn't Molly. Was it Jake, or were there some variables at play that we were unaware of?

Detective Keeler looked up at me and slid the papers into the coat pocket with the flask. "Thank you for your time, Mrs. Carrera. If I could trouble you to provide this Francine's last name and number, it would save me some time."

Wow. That was surprisingly cordial for a man who'd always been terribly rude. But then again, I guess people could turn on the nice when they wanted something.

"I'll call Kat and get it," I promised.

I walked the detective to the door, scooping up my cat so he didn't escape as the man left. Then I stood by my window and watched him drive off.

Stacy Mellomaker *had* been murdered. The police had

three suspects. And I really hoped it wasn't two of them, although I had nothing against the sexy personal trainer.

My cell phone buzzed in my pocket and I nearly dropped Taco. He let out an irritated *meow* and I sat him down, rushing to pull the phone out of my pocket before it went to voice mail.

"Hello?" I didn't recognize the number and hoped I hadn't almost dropped my cat in a rush to answer a replacement window salesperson.

"Hi, this is Francine Bowman. Kat Lars left me a message to call you?"

Bowman. That was her name. And now I had her number to give to Detective Keeler. Kat had clearly turned into an amateur detective and decided to take the initiative on the matter of the third flask.

"Thank you for calling," I told her. "I was hoping I could ask you a few questions about the flask you, Stacy, and Kat got from Pastor Tim at the church."

"The flask?" She laughed. "Now that was funny. Can you imagine sending engraved flasks to a church? I grabbed one on a whim, but I obviously don't need a flask as I'm pregnant, and I'm not much of an alcohol drinker anyway. I gave mine to Molly at the gym. I know she's not twenty-one yet, but it had a bunch of rhinestones and fake gems on it. I thought a young person would enjoy something like that."

"Molly?" My heart sank. It was Molly. How could I have been so wrong about someone? How could she have fooled me like that?

"Molly. She does the towels and stocks the supplies at Forever Fitness. She's such a nice girl. She's really protective of that brother of hers. They're twins, but she always seems older, you know? I think he might have a minor developmental issue. Totally sweet guy, but always seemed kinda clueless. Molly's got a more realistic idea of who people really are underneath it all. I worry that boy is going to go out west like he keeps saying and get taken advantage of. He's so beautiful, so sweet…"

"Were there any other flasks?" I asked, crossing my fingers. "Kat said three, but maybe there was one more she forgot about."

"Just the three. Kat and I and Stacy took them, although I think Stacy is the only one who actually used hers. The woman was a functioning alcoholic. Bloody Marys and mimosas for brunch, wine and mixed drinks with lunch, happy hour, wine with dinner, after dinner drinks. She wrapped it all up like she was some nineteen-forties film star drinking her way through the day, but it was a problem. I caught her in the gym bathroom once emptying a mini of vodka into a smoothie, and she took to carrying that flask around with her. I saw it in her purse more times than I can count."

"What about Jake?" I asked, somehow wanting Molly to not be the murderer. Maybe Molly had given the flask to Jake since she was underage. Although why she would think Jake would want a blingy flask was beyond me.

"Jake? He's good looking, flatters all the women. He's a good trainer, but sleazy in my opinion. Stacy latched on him the moment she joined the gym. I wouldn't have been surprised if they'd had a thing going on all these years."

Could Jake have been angry that his sugar mama was leaving him to run off with a younger man? Or had I been wrong about Molly and she was both a murderer and a better actor than her brother?

CHAPTER 15

On the way to the gym the next morning, I called Detective Keeler and left a message saying that I'd spoken to Francine, had information on the flask, and that I'd meet him at noon at my office. I know I probably should have just turned the whole thing over to him, but I wanted to give Molly a chance to explain what had happened—and I wanted her to accompany me to give her story to the police voluntarily rather than being hauled out of work and in for questioning.

Getting a word in with Molly was a bit difficult because the girl was obviously avoiding me. After a few attempts, I finally headed in to my session with Jake.

I'd been so sore from yesterday's session that I'd had to take some pain reliever before coming in. Today was even tougher with the personal trainer pushing me farther than I'd ever thought possible. He was just as flirty and handsy as he was yesterday, and although normally his attentions would be flattering, I was far too sweaty and in pain to appreciate them. Actually, at one point I wished he'd just cut it out and leave me to my agony of squats and leg presses.

I somehow convinced him to wrap up early and snuck around trying to catch Molly. Finally, I was able to corner her in the back room where Jake had measured me the day before.

"I don't want to talk to you," she informed me as she yanked some laundry bags from the lockers and tossed them into a cart.

"You *need* to talk to me." I followed her as she wheeled the cart from the room to the members' locker area. "Detective Keeler from the Milford Police Department came by my house yesterday. The autopsy results are in and they're ruling Stacy Mellomaker's death a homicide. Someone slipped her drugs. Her death wasn't an accidental overdose."

Molly hesitated a split second, then continued opening lockers and tossing laundry bags into her cart. "I had nothing to do with it. I didn't kill her."

I trailed after her as she pushed the cart through the locker room and down a hall. "It's unlikely that the drugs were in her food or drink. Due to the timing and witnesses, it seems that someone dosed liquor in a flask."

Molly pushed the cart through a back "Employees Only" door and I followed, watching as she began to dump the contents of the laundry bags into a giant industrial-sized washer.

"It wasn't me. If she had a flask with booze in it, then who's to say someone at her house didn't put the drugs in, like her husband? Or a friend? It could have been spiked any time, even days before that bingo game."

"These were very strong drugs. They would have taken effect fast. She was drinking from the flask early in the night and was fine, so it's looking like they were put there when we'd gotten up to go get dinner."

Molly stopped and turned to face me, two laundry bags in her hand.

"It wasn't me." Her voice quavered with the words.

"While we were up getting food, someone came by and swapped the flasks. There wasn't time for them to snatch her flask, go somewhere unseen to put the drugs in, then return it to her purse. Someone had an identical flask. Someone knew what sort of booze Stacy Mellomaker drank. Someone swapped the flask she'd been drinking from earlier with one that had drugs in it, and the only time Stacy was away from her table long enough for them to do it was while we were getting food."

The woman's lips quivered. Tears sparkled in her eyes. "It wasn't me. I don't know what booze she drinks. I don't have a flask."

"But you do. You have the exact same flask that Stacy had. Francine gave it to you. There were three flasks. We have one that belonged to Kat Lars, and it's never been used. That leaves two flasks—Stacy's and the one Francine gave you. You were seen arguing with Stacy. It's well known that she hated you. You had reason to want her dead—to keep her away from your brother. You were there at bingo that night and you were in possession of a flask that the police think is the murder weapon. Molly, this is serious."

She dropped the bags to the floor and burst into tears. "That flask went missing weeks ago. I put it in my locker when Francine gave it to me, and a few days later I realized it was gone. I didn't think anything of it at the time. I didn't care, since I don't drink anyway. It wasn't me."

I believed her, but I wasn't sure Detective Keeler would. "Who saw Francine give the flask to you? Who knew you had it?"

She sniffed and wiped her eyes on her sleeve. "Everyone. It was by the membership desk in the middle of the main gym. We were having a little baby shower thing for Francine that the members and club put together, and everyone was there. When she was packing up the presents and getting ready to leave, she pulled it out of her purse and gave it to me. Everyone laughed because she told me I'd need to wait until I was twenty-one to use it."

Great. This was not narrowing down the suspect pool at all. "Is there any record of who was there at the baby shower?" I asked.

She nodded. "There's timesheets for the employees. And the club can pull the swipes for the day. That will show who came in and used their key fob. But lots of people don't bother, and people don't scan out when they leave."

Keeler would be in a better position to get that information than I would be. "Okay. Here's how this needs to go. You need to come with me to meet with the detective at noon. Tell him everything you've told me. Don't leave anything out. It's better if you go to him then if he has to find you and bring you in."

Her eyes widened. "He'd come here? They'd fire me if the police showed up for me."

"That's why it's important for you to come meet with him. Can you get off work around eleven-thirty?"

She looked up at the clock. "I guess I have to. Amy can finish up with the laundry for me. She comes in at one."

I wanted to reassure her. I wanted to tell her that it was all going to be okay. But I couldn't guarantee that, and the evidence did point to her. The only thing in her favor right now was that no one had found either flask. With them both missing, there might not be enough for the police to charge her.

"Let me get the rest of this in the washer, then I'll go." Molly grabbed a bag out of the cart and pulled open the drawstring top. As she went to dump the contents into the washer, the bag clunked against the side of the machine.

With a frown, she upended it onto the floor, and there among all the towels and washcloths were two flasks.

Two flasks covered with rhinestones and engraved with the name Crossroads Community Church.

* * *

MOLLY HANDED the laundry bag to Detective Keeler, her hands shaking. She'd gone over her story with tears streaming down her face and panic in her voice.

"Mrs. Carrera and I put all the laundry back in the bag along with the two flasks," she told him. "I don't know if there's anything on the towels that will help. Maybe the flasks have fingerprints or DNA or something on them. Oh, God. They probably have my fingerprints and DNA, too. I tried to be careful and use the towels to handle them, but I might have touched them."

I reached out and gave Molly a quick hug. She was an emotional wreck and I was worried that Detective Keeler would be just as harsh and grumpy with her as he'd always been with me.

I shouldn't have worried. The detective gave her a smile that was downright kind.

"How did you know Mrs. Mellomaker was going to be at bingo that night, Molly?" he asked, his voice deep and soothing.

"She was in the members' locker room Tuesday morning, telling Mrs. Houck that she was going to bingo that evening. She was making fun of it, saying how much she hated bingo and that it was trailer trash gambling like scratch-offs. Mrs. Houck asked her why she was going, and Mrs. Mellomaker said she had some unfinished business to take care of and wanted to do it in a public place. She said it would be the last time she ever played bingo if she could help it."

Detective Keeler patted her on the arm. "And when you sat down to talk to her that night at bingo, she told you that she was leaving her husband and going to California with your brother?"

Molly's eyes sparked with renewed tears and her jaw clenched. "He's eighteen and she's *old*. He's not...he doesn't always take care when it comes to people who might not have his best interests in mind. I don't like the idea of him going out to California, but I especially didn't like him going with that nasty, shallow, witch of a woman."

Keeler nodded sympathetically. "And your brother has special needs? He's developmentally disabled?"

"No!" She bit her lip, looking worried at her outburst. "I mean, everyone says that, but he's *not* disabled. He graduated high school. He took all the same classes as we did, he had an IEP from grade school on, but lots of kids have those. He just...he learns things slower than others and he isn't very good at judging people's motivations. He thinks everyone is kind and nice and he's always got a sunny outlook on life. Bad stuff just rolls off him like water off a duck's back. He doesn't notice it. If someone's mean to him, it doesn't even register. He's not street smart. People have conned him out of money or things before with some stupid sob story and he just swallows it hook, line, and sinker."

"And you'd confronted Mrs. Mellomaker several times about her involvement with your brother." Detective Keeler made a "tsk" sound. "I would have done the same in your shoes."

Molly blinked back tears. "I didn't kill her. I just wanted her to leave my brother alone and go seduce some other man instead. When she told me at bingo that she was leaving her husband, that he was giving her money and that she was going to make Hunter a star, I kinda gave up. I'd be there for him if she ditched him, but he's a grown man. I can't stop him, and I got the feeling that she was sincere—at least for the time being."

"I'm assuming that a member of the gym or another employee took that flask from your locker," he mused. "Do you have any idea which locker that bag might have come from?"

Molly shook her head. "I know it looks bad. I know it looks like I did it. I swear it wasn't me."

He patted her on the arm again. "If you were smart enough to plan all this out, then I doubt you would have dumped the laundry bag with the flasks onto the floor right in front of Mrs. Carrera. Now tell me how you collect these bags, Molly. How often and where you gather them from."

Molly took a deep breath. "Most time people just drop their towels and washcloths on the floor, and I go around and pick them up throughout the day and put them in a bag over in the members' locker room. When it's full, I stick it in one of the lockers and every two days I put it all in the wash. Once a week I go through all the unlocked lockers and gather any bags. Those usually aren't towels from the shower and the locker room, but ones from the weight area and the workout rooms. The instructors usually gather them and stick them in a bag, then when the bag is full, they'll just put it out of the way in an empty locker so the place doesn't look messy or get smelly. I do a sweep Sunday morning and gather all those up."

"Then am I right in assuming these bags were probably from staff and not members?"

Molly wrinkled her nose. "Probably. But if it was a long-time member, then they could have known about our process and might have shoved the flasks in one of the bags."

"That makes sense." Keeler nodded. "So, you were collecting the laundry bags. You'd already put the contents of some in the washer. Given how far down this bag was in the cart, where do you think it might have come from?"

She thought for a moment. "Maybe the weight room? I went through the spin room and the yoga studio first, so those were at the bottom. Then the weight room. Then I went through the womens' locker room in case there was anything there. I always figure I might as well wash all the towels if I'm gonna do laundry."

"And the little room where Jake does his measurements," I reminded her. "That's where I caught up with you this morning. You were pulling a bag from the lockers there."

She blinked in surprise. "Yeah, I'd forgotten about that. Jake doesn't keep dirty laundry in there. He takes it directly to the laundry. I usually don't even go through there, but today I figured I might as well check all the lockers and be thorough."

Jake. Suddenly everything clicked together, and someone who'd I'd always thought might be a suspect moved to the front of my guilty list. Six years he'd worked with Stacy Mellomaker. Six years of training sessions and more. How much money *was* Stacy paying her lover? And it was all drying up because she was leaving to run off with someone else. All the personal training fees. All the money under the table for one-on-one sessions. All the gifts and cash a wealthy woman would pay her lover to ensure his services and his silence.

Stacy Mellomaker had promised Hunter a whole lot of things. What if she'd promised Jake a whole lot of things as well? Six years was a long time to have a relationship with someone, a long time to wait for the expected payoff.

He'd have access to Molly's flask. He was at the VFW. He knew what booze Stacy drank. What perfect revenge to have her die sprawled across a bathroom floor in a very public venue.

I pulled a twenty out of my purse. "Molly, would you run down to the corner and get us coffee? I'm sure we could all use some caffeine right now."

Molly glanced over at the coffee maker right next to us, then nodded. "Yes, ma'am. I'll be right back."

Smart girl. She knew I wanted a few words with Detective Keeler in private, and I was grateful that she finally trusted me enough to let me handle this in her absence. I waited until she'd left then turned to the detective.

"It's Jake."

His demeanor shifted from caring and supportive to eye-rolling skeptic. "Really? Tell me why you think it's the personal trainer."

"Six years Stacy Mellomaker had been paying him for personal training sessions and probably a whole lot more. That was all about to end, and I have a feeling Stacy had been just as excited about her relationship with Jake in the beginning as she was with Hunter. Revenge for getting ditched. He was there. It was a public place where she could give him the shove off and maybe a final check. He'd have known what booze she kept in her flask and the flask itself. He was probably there when Francine gave the other flask to Molly. He'd have known it was the same as Stacy's. And by then he probably suspected he was being replaced by a younger model."

"That's a lot of 'if,'" Keeler drawled. "How do you know he wasn't perfectly okay with what he knew would be a temporary arrangement? And where did he get the drugs? There's no proof that Stacy arranged to meet him there, that she was paying him for anything more than professional personal training services through the gym. There's no proof that they had anything sexual going on between them. Or proof that he stole the flask from Molly. This could have been any number of people who had access to the gym and were either at the bingo hall or popped in for a quick swap of the flask.

And when it comes down to it, we don't even know for sure if the flask is the vehicle used to drug Mrs. Mellomaker."

I sighed, knowing he was right. "Is he going to get away with it?"

Detective Keeler shot me a rare smile. "Patience and persistence is the name of this game, Mrs. Carrera. I'll have the flasks tested and trust me, even if he washed them out with bleach, we'll find some drug and alcohol residue. And with luck, we'll find DNA and fingerprints. Criminals are not often as smart or as thorough as they think. If we can get proof that there were drugs in one flask and the same booze in both, and that Mrs. Mellomaker drank from both of them, that's a start. If we can find a partial print from this Jake, that's an even better start. Then we can begin to build a case and find proof of a relationship, proof that this Jake may have had reason to want revenge. Jumping to conclusions and acting too fast threatens our ability to put the killer behind bars. Let the professionals handle this, Mrs. Carrera."

"I am a professional," I shot back. He was right, though. What he wasn't right about was the help I could provide. I did have a paying client I needed to satisfy, and she would want her sister's killer to pay for his crime.

Detective Keeler stood. "Just don't get trapped in any dumpsters, Mrs. Carrera. Okay?"

I held up a hand. "I promise."

The detective left. I sat and stared at my computer for a few moments, waiting for Molly to arrive. When she came back, she was carrying three coffees.

"Where's Detective Keeler?" She looked around like she expected him to jump out from under a desk and cuff her.

"Gone." It was Sunday. I'd gone to the gym. I should be home knitting, or petting my cat, or finishing up the scarf I was knitting, or playing Mario Kart with Henry, or looking at cake recipes with Madison.

"Who do you think killed Stacy Mellomaker?" I asked Molly.

She set her jaw. "Jake. I'm pretty sure they were having a sugar-momma arrangement going on for years. I'm pretty sure he is the type of guy who'd be pissed that was coming to an end, especially with him pushing thirty."

"We need proof of that—of the relationship as well as that he was getting paid. *And* that he was the sort of man who'd want revenge over Stacy dumping him for an eighteen-year-old."

She nodded.

"We need proof that he had access to the drugs. Except I don't know yet exactly what drugs were used to kill Stacy."

"How do we get all that?" Molly asked.

I gestured for the woman to wheel a chair over to my desk. "Where you get everything these days. The internet."

CHAPTER 16

One thing I'd learned from my Sunday afternoon overtime work with Molly was that the girl was smart and that she caught on fast. We'd quickly discovered where Jake lived, who his family was, what high school he'd gone to and that he posted more Instagram workout pictures than I could ever imagine. The guy had thirty thousand Instagram followers, all of them commenting on his pics about his workout routine and supplements. Molly was the one who pointed out from Jake's posts that he was probably getting sponsorship money as an influencer due to the regular product endorsements and coupon codes in his posts.

He also played off the fact that he was single and "available," getting all sorts of female attention on his posts. All that was carefully managed with the skill of someone who was used to keeping women interested and enthused without crossing the line into something more personal.

There was nothing in any of his social media posts or in readily available records that hinted at any relationship with Stacy Mellomaker, though. With a quick warning to Molly concerning the ethics of what I was about to do, I used Jake's full name, birth date, and address from public records to pull a credit report and FICO score.

The guy had money, that much was clear. Credit cards. Decent credit score. On intuition, I pulled up the property tax records and typed in his address, thrilled to find what I'd suspected.

"Bingo," I told Molly. Jake's condo was owned by Stacy Mellomaker. It had been bought six years ago. And I had no doubt that she'd intended to sell it and add to the funds she would need to leave Gus and head out west with Hunter.

Before I finished up for the day, I called Brenda, asking to move up our meeting Monday morning and asking if she could manage to obtain a few things for me beforehand.

I'd dropped Molly off at her car at the gym right around dinner time, then headed home to see the kids off to their Mom's. They'd be back for Thanksgiving, but I was starting to ache over the week without them almost as much as Judge Beck did.

That night I holed up in the dining room, trying to get as many skip traces done as I could while Judge Beck was silently working across from me.

The next morning, I skipped the expensive gym and did yoga with Daisy, calling J.T. to let him know I had a few meetings before I'd be in to the office.

Heading straight to the coffee shop, I got a latte and waited. Brenda wandered in bundled up from the cold, a red-striped shopping bag in her hand.

"Here's the last three years." She handed me a huge stack of bank statements with Stacy's login and password written in black ink at the top. "I've also got her cell phone, unlocked and fully charged. Oh, and here's the autopsy details."

I grinned. "I can't believe you got these."

"It helps that Gus is buddies with the Chief of Police, and

that he's eager to make sure he doesn't end up a suspect now that Stacy's death is considered a homicide." She sat down across from me. "I'm guessing I have you to thank for that?"

"Actually, the autopsy was the catalyst. They would have jump-started the official investigation even without my involvement," I grudgingly admitted. "But I'd like to think the police are closer to nailing down key suspects because of the work I've put in."

"Well, I appreciate your effort. Do I need to give you any more money?"

I quickly tallied the hours I'd put in and lied. "No, we're good still. I'll let you know if we need anything more, but I think we'll be okay with the retainer you paid."

I would make a terrible business owner. J.T. would have a fit if he'd heard me just now, but I really didn't want to charge Brenda any extra than I had to. It was more important to me to see justice served.

She nodded and reached out to shake my hand. "I've really got to run then. The viewing is tomorrow, and I'm helping with Sheyanne as well as going through Stacy's clothes and other effects. Gus wants them gone."

I thought about the bingo baskets and how he hadn't wanted anything to do with them. It was like he was erasing Stacy from his life. I couldn't blame his lack of grief. He'd made a mistake and had stayed the course for duty and responsibility, but Stacy's passing wasn't cause for sadness, only regret, as he'd said. Gus had kept his first wife's picture, clung to the memories of their life together. He wouldn't want to do so with Stacy. He probably only wanted to forget their life together. Well, except for Sheyanne, that is.

"What are you planning to do with her things?" I asked. "Donate them?"

She snorted. "Yeah. Like I'm going to give Luis Vuitton purses and Prada shoes to Goodwill."

Okay. I guess that meant she was keeping or selling it all. Suddenly I was glad of the relationship Eli and I had. I'd never had any siblings, nor had Eli, but I certainly hoped if we did, they wouldn't be like this. I watched Brenda leave, gathered up all her stuff, then went to my second appointment of the morning, armed with the very thing I hoped would bring us closer to an answer in who killed Stacy Mellomaker—the lab report.

* * *

I HANDED Doctor Bern the autopsy report and the hospital notes. Then I sat and waited while he read, the only noise the flipping of pages and Tom's occasional clearing of his throat.

"So?" I asked once he finished and handed the files back to me in a neat stack.

"Based on the hospital notes, I would have thought she was a closet junkie. You'd be shocked about the functioning addicts in our society, especially ones with enough wealth to cover it up."

"But?"

"But this." He pointed to a portion of the autopsy report. "That's a really high concentration of morphine. Addicts don't go straight from Oxycodone pills to that. I would have expected to see signs of heroin use first."

"And there were none," I commented.

"So that means either she was an addict, and someone slipped her a lethal dose in what she thought was a prescription strength Percocet or she wasn't an addict and the killer had access to what was probably liquid morphine."

"She didn't have any track marks. That bottle of hydrocodone was from a prescription filled over a year ago and more than half full when the EMTs took it out of her purse. Does that sound like an addict to you?" I asked.

"No," Tom admitted. "But if I was just looking at the bloodwork, I'd have expected that she was either a heavy heroin user or someone in the final stages of cancer."

I blinked at his last comment then looked down at the file again. "Cancer?"

"That amount of morphine is a near-death comfort care dose, Kay. That's what we give people who are so far along that we don't expect them to live more than a week or two max. They're usually in hospice care, down to seventy pounds, and on the edge of organ failure. That level of dosage would keep them from suffering until they pass. Anyone else taking that would die, but cancer patients at that stage have generally built up a tolerance to pain management drugs and require the high levels. A healthy, fit, thirty-five-year-old woman would not be on that level of morphine. And she shouldn't be taking it recreationally at that level unless she'd been using for years and years with increasingly high dosages. An addict able to tolerate that amount of morphine recreationally wouldn't have been able to hide her addiction. She'd be clearly on something, even when she wasn't passed out."

"And you said liquid?"

"Liquid." Tom nodded. "Again, I'm looking at this through the lens of my oncology practice, but we often prescribe liquid morphine for late-stage cancer patients. Some of them can no longer swallow pills, and while we have a patch that delivers a consistent dose, liquid morphine taken in small doses on a regular schedule does wonders in relieving the pain these patients have."

"Is that available on the street?" I still couldn't quite wrap my head around how a killer could have gotten hold of this.

"Anything is available on the street." Tom rolled his eyes. "Anything. But heroin and fentanyl are easier to get than this. The morphine in the report? It's medical grade. It's not some crap brought up from South America and diluted in a back room."

"So the killer could have gotten it on the street, but it isn't likely?" I asked.

He nodded. "Let's just say that if the killer got it on the street, then he's got connections either in at-home nursing care or through the hospice."

"Not the hospital?" Surely the hospital had these medicines as well.

"Probably not. There are some rigid controls about these medicines at the hospital. I'm not saying someone couldn't sneak out a bottle, but it would be difficult, and I can guarantee they'd get caught the second time if they managed to even get away with it once. But remember those hospice patients I was mentioning? Let's just say there are a lot of powerful drugs that don't necessarily get turned in when those patients die. And usually the supply is generous enough that if an unscrupulous nurse or care worker were to take some, it might not be noticed. Especially in a home care setting. Family coming and going. The concern over having enough drugs if the pain becomes intolerable in the middle of the night on a weekend."

I left Tom Bern and headed in to the office. The ghost beside me changed the radio channels, and as I listened to "Hey Joe" by Jimi Hendrix, I thought through the case. I was positive Jake was the killer but where would he have gotten palliative care levels of morphine? Hopefully the bank statements and the cell phone Brenda had given me would reveal that Stacy and Jake had a connection, but a long-lasting love affair wasn't enough for Detective Keeler to charge him for murder.

J.T. was already in, invoicing and sending out reports on the skip trace files I'd completed and sitting in my chair in front of my computer was Molly.

"Hi." She stood as I came in, casting a nervous glance over at J.T. "I wondered if I could help. I'm off work today and thought maybe I could go through files or look things up on my laptop."

I glanced over at J.T., who looked up and gave me a nod. "You did say you needed help. I told her I'd pay her ten dollars an hour for any assistance today, and if she works out, maybe this could wind up being a part time job."

I'll admit after yesterday's work, I had thought maybe Molly would be the perfect addition to our office. She was smart, motivated, and I was sure I could quickly train her how to do the skip trace work. Of course, we'd need to make sure she didn't end up being charged for Stacy Mellomaker's murder first.

"Is that something you'd want?" I asked Molly.

She nodded. "Heck, yeah. This would be a whole lot more interesting than cleaning up towels and running to get juices for rich women."

"Maybe not," I warned her. "There's a lot of routine computer work involved. Most of your time would be spent doing internet research and writing reports."

"And catching killers," she added excitedly.

"Not a lot of catching killers," I said, even though I'd certainly done my fair share of that this year. "And you'd be running down to the courthouse now and then to get files or drop things off in addition to handling basic skip trace work."

"I'll take it," she said with a grin. "Now what do I do first? Stakeout Jake's house? Break into his locker at the gym and search it? Wiretap his car?"

I looked at the stack of bank statements and decided I'd be better suited to go through those. "How about you pull out your laptop and start running an internet search on Jake. Everything. Mentions in newspapers, social media accounts, pictures that he was tagged in. Take notes about everything you find and see if you can come up with anything that might point to a relationship with Stacy Mellomaker, or him having access to drugs like heroin or morphine."

"Like a friend that was arrested for dealing?" she asked.

"Exactly."

Molly switched to the guest chair and pulled out her laptop, settling in at a little side table. If this worked out, we'd need to get her a desk. If it worked out, that is. I was pretty sure after a day of boring internet searches, she'd be ready to go back to the health club.

I sat down and started with Stacy's cell phone. The woman had made it ridiculously easy. Jake was listed in her contacts, as well as Dennis and Hunter. With Hunter, she'd mostly sent texts, and I was thrilled to see that none of them included naked self-ies. The texts had started a month ago and had increased over the last two weeks. It seemed the woman was infatuated with him, and she was indeed promising him the moon and the stars.

There had been no recent contact with Dennis, and the cell records on the phone went back for three months. There were quite a few phone calls made to Jake, tapering off in the last few weeks with the final one the day of Stacy's death.

There had either been no text messages to Jake, or they'd been wiped clean. Well, no text messages except for one. Tuesday at six in the evening, she'd sent one to him that simply stated, "I'm here."

I set the phone aside, making a mental note to take it to Detective Keeler later today, then I got started on the bank statements. That's when I hit pay dirt. Stacy's bank accounts showed regular checks made out to Jake. PT checks should have gone to the gym, but these were directly to him and totaling up to nearly six thousand a month.

And the checks stopped last month.

Stacy had bought the condo he was living in. She'd been supporting him. Jake worked at the gym where the flasks had been found. He would have known what whisky she drank. He would have access to steal the other flask Francine gave Molly. And he had motive – had Stacy promised him the same things she'd promised Hunter? Had six years of being led on with promises of a wealthy divorcee been smashed when Stacy announced she was ditching him and running off with Hunter?

He was at the bingo night. And judging from the last text, Jake was the unfinished business Stacy said she mentioned. Had she arranged to talk to him there and give him the same speech she'd given Molly? Had he seen it coming and prepared a bit of revenge?

The only thing missing was access to the drugs. Where would Jake have gotten morphine?

"I think I've got something." Molly spun her chair around to face me. "I couldn't come up with anything on the internet that tied Jake to Mrs. Mellomaker, but I did find out that his grandmother died about a month ago."

I slowly shook my head, not making the connection.

"In the obituary, it said in lieu of flowers, the family had requested donations to cancer research as well as the local hospice." She bounced excitedly. "Wouldn't his grandmother have been on some serious painkillers if she'd had cancer? What if Jake slipped a few into his pocket when he was visiting her before she died?"

I remembered my conversation with Tom. "Liquid morphine. The autopsy showed a really high dose of morphine in Stacy's system, and my oncologist friend said that level would be used as pain relief for people dying of cancer—people who were in hospice care."

"Maybe after she died, Jake took an unfinished bottle of

morphine," Molly suggested. "I'm sure nobody would have noticed if it went missing."

Having been caretaker of my invalid husband for the last ten years, I knew how a long-term—or even terminal—illness could result in a stockpile of drugs that increased in dosage—a dosage that would be lethal to someone who'd not legally obtained them.

"If she was in home hospice care, they might have had more than just an unfinished bottle," I commented. "There might have been several bottles at the house, just so they wouldn't run out."

Molly nodded. "So, what do we do now? Search his house for the drugs?"

"No," I told her. "We most definitely do not search his house. We take all this over to Detective Keeler, and we let the police do their job."

CHAPTER 17

I stopped by the police station on my way home and dropped off copies of the bank statements with the highlighted portions showing the checks to Jake as well as the cell phone and a report I'd quickly typed up summarizing what I'd found as well as Molly's theory about the grandmother and Jake's possible access to liquid morphine.

Afterward, I went home, took care of Taco, then settled in to work on skip traces. Judge Beck joined me in our dining room/office when he got home a few hours later, and we silently worked until after midnight, making sandwiches and munching on chips when we got hungry. As much as I hated working so late, it was rather nice having the judge across the table from me, also elbow-deep in papers and files. Hopefully J.T. would be as impressed by Molly as I was and would hire her on. It would be wonderful not to have such a huge workload and be able to actually enjoy a relaxing evening once again. Plus, I would love having someone else in the office. J.T. was often out meeting with clients or handling the bail bonds and recovery side of the business, and I got a bit lonely sitting there all by myself from eight to five.

Dragging myself out of bed the next morning, I was actually grateful to be doing yoga with Daisy. Two days in a row of weight training with Jake had left me stiff and sore and having Monday off had only made it worse. Although I felt like I was the most inflexible woman in the world, the yoga practice did loosen up my stiff joints and muscles and gave me a sense of peace I hadn't had in nearly a week.

By the time I strolled into the office, I was feeling pretty good about life. I'd done a good job on the Mellomaker case and felt confident that Detective Keeler would soon be making an arrest. I was nearly caught up on the skip trace files. I was only pleasantly sore and not feeling as if I could hardly manage to bend over and tie my shoes. And the Thanksgiving plans were all coming together. Madison was making what I knew would be an amazing sausage and chestnut stuffing. Judge Beck was bringing some oysters and braving the cold to grill them outside. Daisy had promised her amaretto and pecan sweet potato casserole. Henry had volunteered to help by snapping the fresh green beans and cooking them with a healthy scoop of bacon grease and some chopped ham. J.T. was bringing a few loaves of French bread and the wine.

I was doing the turkey and mashed potatoes as well as the pumpkin pies for dessert. I got a little twinge of nostalgia at the thought. Eli had always taken charge of the turkey, brining it the night before and carefully putting together his "secret" spice mix. He'd get up early and put it in the oven, then carefully baby it throughout the day until it was ready for the table. We'd always invite friends to join us for Thanksgiving—friends without family, those who were single and far away from their parents, friends that had just gone through a divorce and were all alone for the holiday. Eli would present his turkey as if he were one of the three wise men bringing gifts for baby Jesus, and I'd handle the rest with friends bringing side dishes.

But after the accident, that had all changed. Eli couldn't remember what day of the week it was most times, let alone that there was a holiday coming up. Often, I'd put together a little something with a small turkey breast and some pre-made mashed potatoes, but it had only seemed to make him sad—to remind him that the life we'd had was over forever.

This Thanksgiving…it was going to be a lot like what Eli and I had in the old days, except there would be no Eli.

My chest ached at the thought. I was going to do the turkey like he'd always done, down to the spice recipe he'd always thought was so "secret." It was important to me, as if this was an homage to my husband, a thank you for all the years we'd had together.

It seemed like closure and that kind of scared me.

Around noon, I told J.T. that I was probably going to be a bit late back from lunch and headed out to the gym. I knew I didn't have any investigative reason to be there, but the personal training session with Jake was already paid for, and I thought I might as well take advantage of it.

In the locker room, Molly flagged me down, her face flushed with excitement.

"I did it! I did it!"

"Did what?" I shimmied into my yoga tights and carefully hung my work pants in the locker.

"Remember how I searched all those things on the internet yesterday? And how you-know-who's grandmother died? Well, I went over to you-know-who's mother's house this morning on my way into work. I told her that I was from Hospice and was there to express our condolences once more and survey them about the program. Then I reminded her to make sure she took any remaining medicines to the hospital or the sheriff's office for proper disposal because we wanted to make sure they didn't get into the wrong hands or be accidently taken."

I blinked in surprise. "You did what?"

It was actually a brilliant move on her part, but I worried about an eighteen-year-old girl risking herself like this. What if Jake had been there? What if the mother told Jake and described Molly? Any man who was ruthless enough to kill his lover wouldn't think twice about killing a young woman who'd found him out.

Molly beamed. "Wait until you hear the rest. I thought for sure she'd say that they'd forgotten to turn them in, and that they were still in the house, but no. She told me that they had definitely taken the medicines to the sheriff's office—that her son you-know-who had taken them over himself the week after the funeral."

"That would be really easy for Detective Keeler to confirm," I mused. "And if he *didn't* turn in the medicine, then we'd know he could have used it to poison Stacy."

"Even if he turned it in, he might have kept some back," Molly told me. "I looked it up. The sheriff's department keeps track of that stuff since it's a controlled substance. They'd know exactly how much he turned in. And there would be clear records of how much Jake's grandmother was prescribed. There'd be a clear discrepancy."

"Did you tell the police yet?" I asked.

She nodded. "I called on my way in and left a message for that detective."

"Molly, please be careful," I pleaded. "I don't want anything to happen to you. If Ja—you-know-who is really the killer, then he might come after you."

She straightened her shoulders. "I can take care of myself. I've been watching him today, just to make sure he doesn't pull anything or try to skip town. I might park my car across from his condo tonight and keep watch unless the police arrest him today."

"Molly—"

"Hurry up, you've got a session starting now. Don't worry, I'll hang around and watch in case he pulls anything."

I blew out a puff of air and slammed my locker shut. Maybe Molly wasn't cut out for a part time job at our company. But then again, I'd nearly been shot by the mayor, had gotten trapped in a dumpster, and had participated in a car chase through the cemetery, so I guess I couldn't cast stones.

I headed out for my personal training session. Jake was his usual sexy, flattering self, alternating between complimenting me and making me lift far more than I ever thought I could manage. All the while Molly lingered, wiping off the same workout equipment over and over as she glared at the personal trainer.

Midway through my second set of bicep curls, Jake got a call. Giving me an apologetic glance and motioning for me to continue, he answered. I tried to listen while still attempting to maintain my weight routine. Jake answered with a warm, friendly tone, then grew increasingly anxious as the person spoke.

"Yes, of course I did. I'll call them and make sure they know. No, I'll do it." He hung up and turned to me. "I'm really sorry, but I need to cut our session short. Next week I'll give you an extra on the house."

Without waiting for my answer, he spun around and headed for the little room where he'd done my measurements. Molly followed him. I quickly racked the dumbbells and tried to catch up. As I turned the corner, I saw Jake in the room, flinging open one of the locker doors.

"It's not there," Molly told him. "I took it and gave it to the police."

No. *No!* I put on some speed, but Molly's loud voice was drawing a crowd of other gym patrons and I had to weave through them.

"You killed her. You stole the flask from me, filled it with her booze of choice, and added liquid morphine that had been prescribed for your grandmother." She walked across the room and poked a finger into Jake's chest. "I didn't like her, but I wouldn't have killed her. You did. You're a murderer."

"I don't know what you're talking about," Jake snarled. He turned around and opened another locker, pulling something off the top shelf.

"The police are investigating. The autopsy ruled Stacy's death a murder. "

"Molly," I warned, trying to push through the crowd that had gathered at the doorway.

"She was given a fatal dose of liquid morphine in a flask that was switched with hers," Molly continued. "I found both flasks in that locker, and they've got your fingerprints on them. She was ditching you and the money-train was coming to an end, so you killed her."

Jake spun around and grabbed Molly, pulling her against his chest and placing a knife at her throat. "Out of the way. Everyone move out of the way and let me go. I'll kill her if you don't let me go."

I caught my breath, terrified for the young woman. Her eyes met mine, but instead of fear, I saw that steely determined look I'd come to realize was who Molly really was.

She slumped, her entire weight against Jake's arm. His grip relaxed in surprise, the knife nicking her jaw as she slid through his grip. He tightened before her head slid through, bringing the knife back up to her neck.

That was when Molly twisted, driving her fist into the man's crotch.

The man shrieked and dropped like a stone, the knife clattering to the floor. The crowd of members rushed in, tackling Jake. Three women sat on his chest while two others grabbed measuring tapes and began to tie him up. Behind me I heard Ruth talking to the police.

I ran forward, kneeling to tend to Molly. The cut on her jaw was bleeding profusely as was another across the lower part of her neck. Grabbing a towel, I held it to the more serious wound, applying pressure.

"I'm okay," she told me, her smile wavering a bit. "I might need a stitch or two, but I'm okay. I'm not supermodel gorgeous like Hunter. A few scars won't matter."

I smoothed her hair, keeping the towel on her neck. "You're just as gorgeous as your brother. You're smart, and gutsy, and I think you've got a part time job at an investigation firm as long as you promise not to do this sort of thing ever again."

This time her smile held firm. "This coming from the woman who got trapped in a dumpster? I want this job, but no promises, Mrs. Carrera. No promises."

I smiled back. "Fair enough. I'll have to talk to J.T. but let me prematurely welcome you to Pierson Investigative and Recovery Services, Molly."

CHAPTER 18

I walked in with the turkey on a platter. Everyone watched with the sort of reverence they would have given if they'd been observing one of the three kings presenting a gift to baby Jesus.

"That. Smells. Amazing." Henry held up a fork and knife.

A shadow materialized in the corner of the room, and I could swear that he nodded in agreement. The whole day had been a sort of final mourning for me. I'd brined the turkey overnight, then got up before dawn when the house was still asleep to season it and put it in the oven. All day I'd babied that turkey. I'd watched over it while Heather dropped the kids off, while J.T. and Daisy arrived, while Judge Beck went out to put the oysters on the grill. They'd all socialized in the parlor while I'd cooked, refusing any offer to assist. Henry and Madison set the table. We put all the food out. And this last dish, the pièce de résistance, was the turkey.

"Nice job, Kay," J.T. said.

I sat the platter in a place of honor, giving a quick glance over to the shadow in the corner of the room before I sat.

"Madison, will you give the blessing?" Judge Beck asked.

We all bowed our heads, hands clasped in our laps.

"Thank you, Lord, for the bounty on our table. Thank you for the warmth of our house and the sheltering roof over our head. Thank you for the love of friends and family and for our continued health." She shot her father a wicked glance. "And thank you for the 'A' on my calculus exam. In Jesus name we pray, amen."

"Amen," we all responded, everyone placing their napkins into their laps as if we were part of some synchronized dance.

"That calculus grade is due to your hard work, Madison," Judge Beck commented. "Although I appreciate your giving thanks to God, don't deny the time and effort you put into that achievement."

Madison flushed and Henry snorted.

"I aced my history test, not that anyone cares. Guess I should be thanking God for that one, too."

"We all care, Henry," I told the boy. "And all that history homework will come in handy when we play trivia later tonight."

Henry gave a fist-pump and grabbed the bowl of mashed potatoes. The food made a circuit around the table and I noticed J.T. and Daisy leaning close together, their hands touching as they passed the dishes.

"So, what do you think about Molly?" I asked my boss.

"She's hired," J.T. announced without hesitation. "I'll give her a call tomorrow and let her know."

The young woman had only needed two stitches on her jaw and four on the lower part of her neck. No doubt she was home right now, enjoying turkey and stuffing with her mother and brother and waiting anxiously for a call about whether she had a new job or not.

"This sausage and chestnut stuffing is amazing, Madison,"

Daisy said. "You've got a career as a chef ahead of you, I can tell."

The girl smiled. "Thanks, but I've been thinking of maybe studying law instead."

I glanced over and saw that the judge was practically glowing at her statement. I knew he was supportive of his children regardless of what career path they chose, but he not-so-secretly hoped that one of his kids would follow his path into law.

"Does everyone have their Christmas shopping done?" J.T. asked.

We all groaned. None of us had been able to spare a day for shopping. It was increasingly looking like all our gifts would be bought after hours on the internet.

"Maybe we should do some Black Friday shopping," Madison commented. "I've always wanted to do that."

"Are you kidding?" Henry asked. "You have to bring your sleeping bag and camp out at some of those things. That's insane."

"Only if you want the premium sale item," Daisy told him. "If you get up at three or four and go stand in line, you can get a lot of really awesome deals."

I scooped two grilled oysters onto my plate and passed the platter on. "If you really want to go, I'm game. Make a list of where you want to shop, and we'll get up early and head out."

"Really?" Madison's eyes gleamed. "I'll make a list. I'll bet I can get all my Christmas shopping done in one day."

"Deal." I stood and began to carve the turkey, looking over at the shadow in the corner of the room.

This is for you, Eli. I love you. I'll always love you. I'll never forget you, but I might live for another twenty or thirty years and I can't live those years in mourning. We had an amazing life together. And I know you want the rest of my years to be just as amazing, even if those years are without you.

The shadow shimmered and vanished, and a tear rolled down my cheek.

"Are you okay, Kay?" Judge Beck asked.

I nodded, pushing aside the weird mix of sorrow and nostalgia and a guilty kind of joy. "I'm fine. I'm just happy," I told him.

And I realized that I was. I really was happy. And that happiness in no way was disrespectful of the love I'd felt for my husband or the sadness I'd felt over his loss.

I was happy.

*I*t was freezing cold at three o'clock in the morning when I climbed into my vehicle with a thermos of coffee in my hand. I started the car, shivering as the cold air blew out of the heaters full blast.

Madison ran down the porch steps and toward the car, a fuzzy purple scarf around her neck and a huge purple beanie with a pom-pom on her head. She flung open the passenger door and climbed inside.

That's when I realized there was no longer a ghost in my car.

"Do you have your list?" I asked her.

She waved the paper at me. "Absolutely. And my wallet. Dad gave me some money so I should have enough including my allowance."

I had my wallet too, but I was pretty sure I had less money than Madison for shopping. Although I didn't have as many presents to buy. Most everyone I knew was getting a scarf. I just had to buy a gift for Henry.

And for Judge Beck. What to buy the wealthy man who pretty much had everything?

I put the car in reverse and, as we exited the driveway, I leaned forward to turn on the radio. "What a Wonderful World" by Louis Armstrong filled the air and I smiled.

Because yes, it really was indeed a wonderful world.

ACKNOWLEDGMENTS

Special thanks to Lyndsey Lewellen for cover design and typography, and to Erin Zarro for copyediting.

ABOUT THE AUTHOR

Libby Howard lives in a little house in the woods with her sons and two exuberant bloodhounds. She occasionally knits, occasionally bakes, and occasionally manages to do a load of laundry. Most of her writing is done in a bar where she can combine work with people-watching, a decent micro-brew, and a plate of Old Bay wings.

For more information:
libbyhowardbooks.com/

<u>Locust Point Mystery Series:</u>

The Tell All

Junkyard Man

Antique Secrets

Hometown Hero

A Literary Scandal

Root of All Evil

A Grave Situation

Last Supper

A Midnight Clear

Fire and Ice

www.ingramcontent.com/pod-product-compliance
Lightning Source LLC
Chambersburg PA
CBHW020326110726
47898CB00003B/768